My voice is under control now and other stories

Peter Horn

• KWELA BOOKS •

Acknowledgement:
This collection of short stories has been produced
with the assistance of COSAW Publishing.

Photograph on cover by Annari van der Merwe
Drawing on back cover by Nils Burwitz
Cover design by Nazli Jacobs
Set in 11.5 on 14 pt Times
Printed and bound by National Book Printers,
Drukkery Street, Goodwood, Western Cape

First edition, first printing 1999

ISBN 0-7957-0086-5

Vielleicht aber ist Humanität nichts anderes,
als daß sie das Bewußtsein des Schreckens wachhält,
dessen, was sich nicht mehr gutmachen läßt.

Theodor W. Adorno, *Quasi una fantasia.*
Frankfurt am Main 1963, s.53f

But perhaps humanity is nothing other than
keeping alive the consciousness of the horror of
that which can no longer be made good.

Contents

My voice is under control now

A S IT IS THE CUSTOM among our people I have a hole in my upper lip and a hole in my lower lip, and when my husband is tired of my talking, he inserts a wooden peg through the two holes. These holes are made in our lips in a ceremony called the "opening of the mouth" ceremony at the age of four just after we have begun to talk. During this ceremony an old rhyme is taught to all the girls which says that speech is precious and must be guarded behind closed lips. It goes on to say that our fathers and husbands are the guardians of our speech, and that because speech is so precious it must not be spilled except when our guardians are there and mentally prepared to receive it. To spill our speech into other ears, to engage in idle gossip or senseless prattle while our guardians are preoccupied with other, much more important matters, such as drinking beer with their friends and the worthy ancestors, is not only a waste of this precious substance but a serious disturbance of the harmony of the universe, which is expressed in the custom of men to share their beer with the ruling spirits of the universe, the ancestors, in a solemn and ancient ritual of holy jokes about the curves of women's arses and breasts and the textures of their cunts.

I have not always had this deep understanding of our customs.

I

As a child I was very rebellious and often tore the slender wooden peg from my lips when I had the feeling that I just had to tell my parents and their friends about such important matters as that my puppet's leg had come off and needed mending or that I was bleeding from a cut on my knee when I had fallen in one of our childish games. But my parents guided me steadfastly towards an inner acceptance of our sacred customs, and after a long and nearly endless struggle against my rebelliousness I have now finally accepted our wonderful traditions, so that I myself can now hand them on to my own children.

For children who do not immediately accept the customs of our people our society has a very effective measure: the old rhyme says that she who cannot accept the peg must accept the lock. The lock is a heavy iron contraption which hangs painfully in the holes of our lips, and which so effectively locks them that we can only make weird and crazy sounds of no import. The lock also disfigures the face of the woman who has to wear it for any length of time, and this disfigurement vividly shows for all to see that the woman who wears the lock is loquacious and cannot control her urges to prattle and gossip. The lock can only be opened by the key in the hand of our guardian. I am ashamed to say that I had to wear the lock practically constantly from the age of five to the age of thirty. Even marriage did not teach me the value of speech, even having children did not convert me once and for all from my evil ways and so my young babies were confronted with the appalling spectacle of a mother whose lips had to be secured by the lock while they already cheerfully exercised the self-control of submitting to the peg.

Already at the age of six I was caught by my elder sister when I wanted to seduce some of my friends into getting rid of their pegs and indulging in a session of wild and uncontrolled speaking. I had indicated to them that we would meet near the brook just outside our village where the overhanging trees shielded us effectively from the view of our elders. As everybody was very busy on that day preparing for the festival of the naked ancestors, which is celebrated each year at the first full moon after the spring rains and attended by all the men of the village, but for which the women of the village have to prepare enormous amounts of food and drink, we succeeded in slinking away from the control of our guardians and assembling in the cool, shady and secluded spot near the river.

When I took the peg out of my lips, all the other children gasped at my daring and looked at me in admiration mixed with shame and horror. I encouraged them to do the same, and said: Come on, let's gossip! Nobody is going to overhear us!

One of the girls, taking out her peg for a moment, said: But what about the ancestors? Don't they see everything?

I said very daringly: The ancestors are too busy with the festival right now, so none of them will come snooping around here.

This was greeted with a suppressed groan of horror by most of the girls assembled. One did not speak like that of the ancestors! But as I chattered away about the meat and the drink and the music and the dancing and the naked men I had seen throwing stones into the holy holes and about all the interesting and exciting things that were happening in the village right now, the one or the other girl shortly took the peg from her lips and contributed the one or other observation of her own. How the naked men in the great hut of the ancestors had arranged wrestling matches, how they had performed the dance of the insemination of the holy spirit of life, how the mayor had lain drunk in his own vomit for hours before somebody found him, his tongue hanging out and all blue in the face, nearly choked to death. But most of the girls were too terrified to remove their pegs although they of course took in all this exciting talk about our village.

It was then that my sister, who has always been an exemplary girl and never rebelled against the customs of our tradition, discovered us and our transgression and went straight back to my mother and told her about this wicked violation of all the

3

rules which was going on just outside the village. Within minutes my mother and the mothers of all the girls who were with me came running towards the bush and dragged us screaming back to the village. Our fathers were notified in the proper way and they assembled to enquire into this unheard-of thing that young girls of six had come together to gossip next to the river. We were all gathered in a hut which is known as the hut of shame because every woman who has been caught breaking the law of the peg is brought there to be undressed and smeared with the white of shame and then from there led to the tribunal of the broken vow.

Each of us in turn was led to the open place before the hut of the mayor, interrogated and then returned to the hut. In the hut an old woman, called the keeper of the speech, watched over us so as to prevent any more gossiping. When it was my turn I had to repeat word for word what I had said in our gossiping session, and although they must by now have heard it all at least seven times before, after each sentence they broke out in horrified "Oh's" and "Shame's". When we had all been interrogated we were called together before the tribunal and the sentence was read. But first we were given a long and tedious repetition of all the instructions which were part of the "opening of the mouth" ceremony and which clearly set out our duty to be silent unless specifically asked to talk by our guardians. Then the mayor who acted as the judge pronounced sentence: all of us, even the ones who had just listened, were to wear the lock for an entire year. There were horrified shouts from our mothers at this severe sentence. But the mayor said that this unheard-of transgression had to be punished in such a way that the example of the punishment would kill the desire in anybody to imitate us. A short verse about our crime and punishment was even included in the rhymes which were recited at future "opening of the mouth" ceremonies so as to impress on the young girls the seriousness of our offence once and for all.

To my great shame I must confess that I just simply could not control my urges to gossip even after this terrible punishment. While I was never again stupid enough to try and arrange a gossip with a whole crowd of girls, whenever I was not wearing the lock, I succumbed again and again to the desire to tell others about what I had experienced, felt, dreamt, hoped and wanted. And since the other women were aghast at my immorality, not only did I find fewer and fewer friends who were prepared to listen to me, but those on whom I forced my gossip, to whom I exposed myself shamelessly, in order to protect themselves from the lock and from disrepute in the village, began to report my lapses immediately to the guardians.

My worst transgression, however, came at the age of fifteen, and the shame of that event is still burning so vividly in my memory that I can hardly bring myself to talk about it, and it is only so that all can be warned about such immoral behaviour and avoid it in future that I am now recounting this most serious breach of the law of the ancestors ever recorded in our village.

There were very few foreigners ever in our village. An occasional white missionary who attempted to convert us to his strange customs and gave up after a few weeks of oppressive silence from all the women, the occasional trader, who knew however that he was not allowed to gossip with the wives and had to do all his trading with the men. Of course, the ones who sold coloured beads and nicely printed cloth sometimes attempted to break that rule, because it is much easier to persuade a woman to buy such an adornment in exchange for some of the stock of maize she has hidden away in her hut, than a man, who sees these adornments for women as entirely unnecessary. But, of course, such breaches of the rules of conduct were always discovered, at the latest when the unfortunate woman attempted to wear the adornments in public, and were strictly punished by the lock. Nevertheless, it was generally admitted that even meek and mild wives or daughters, who normally submitted to the law of the peg without any resistance, often could not withstand the temptation of a haggling session with one of the traders. So serious was this problem that the guardians at one stage even considered banning the traders from the village. Fortunately that idea was soon buried, since most of the men were too lazy to walk to the far-off town to get their necessary provisions, such as tobacco or yeast for their beer brewing. In any case, they themselves have to adorn their bodies for the various festivals of the ancestors – there are at least fifty of them in the course of the year, with beads, silver armlets and brightly coloured headscarves. On the whole, with the occasional transgression and punishment by the lock, the traders therefore do not pose a serious problem, although their presence is somewhat annoying.

When I found that I had been ostracised by most if not all of the women for my tendency to gossip, and that even the few who were still prepared to listen to me, if not to talk, were so afraid that there were very few chances of a real tension-relieving gossip with them, and since my father was an especially taciturn man by that time, who kept the peg in my lips practically without a break, so depriving me of even the boring conversation with a male guardian, I really became desperate. The long, nearly constant periods which I suffered in the lock added to my frustration and rebelliousness.

I am deeply ashamed to confess that at that time I had begun to hate our ancient and holy customs, I was a more than usually rebellious teenager, I constantly made weird and uncanny noises from behind my lock, which the people around me fortunately could not understand. In any case it was the custom to pretend that women in the lock were not speaking but just making animal noises to which one need pay as little attention as to the screams of the monkeys or the chirping of the birds. Secure behind my lock, which I even began to love in a strange kind of way, I mumbled such blasphemous things as: This entire male society is utterly crazy! It suppresses the most natural urge of all human beings joyfully to talk about all the things that happen to them!

The peg is a torture which men have invented to humiliate wo-men! Why can men gossip as much as they like at their festivals and beer-drinking sessions? The very thought of using such words as "gossip" for the solemn and ancient ritual of holy jokes about the curves of women's arses and breasts and the textures of their cunts today fills me with an unnamed horror. But that, I am ashamed to say, was what I thought at the time. I do not recount it here to encourage young girls and women to follow my shame-ful example but to experience that kind of holy terror which in the end cured me of my afflictions, and the ancestors willing, will keep me on the straight and narrow path through the jungle of life in the future.

Just at that time, when my lock was removed after a lengthy period of over two years, a young white-skinned and fair-haired missionary entered our village. If our men had had their way they would have banned all missionaries from our village, yes, perhaps even have roasted or cooked them at the new moon festival of the angry ancestors. Unfortunately for all of us these meddlesome men apparently had the protection of some very powerful ances-tors somewhere far away, ancestors who in contrast to our own seemed able to protect these men from the wrath of our men far away from their homeland.

Now this missionary belonged to an order which had the out-rageous and strange rule that the men belonging to it had to ex-ercise the same kind of silence as the women in our village. Whether the ancestors of the missionaries believed that such a silent man would be more acceptable in our village because of our law of the peg than one who attempted to talk to the women, I don't know. In reality, however, a man who keeps silent in our village is considered to be effeminate and a weakling, unable to express himself. So this silent missionary was the butt of constant jokes in our village, and the men at the beer-drinking sessions had long conversations about the sexual preferences of a man without a voice: Does he submit to other men to be sexually satis-

7

fied, or does he do it with the wild animals? Even worse things were suggested which are not properly spoken of by a woman, such as that he might even do it to himself with his own hands. The men really had a field day in their sessions of the solemn and ancient ritual of holy jokes.

To me, however, this man seemed to be a fellow sufferer, one who had been condemned by other men to eternal silence, and I felt myself drawn to him inexorably, and I must admit the rumours about his sexual preferences added just that much spice to my fantasies of finding a soulmate. Since at that time I found myself in a rebellion which was so fundamental and which questioned all the wisdom of our community, I was attracted rather than horrified by what at any other time I would have condemned or found ridiculous. So one night I escaped from my parental hut and, in the dark, I entered the missionary's hut. The missionary was on his knees in front of a piece of wood covered in various colours, his hands folded in front of his breast. At first he did not notice me, but when he turned round he looked at me with what seemed great anxiety. He pointed to his mouth, and indicated that it was sealed.

I in turn took the peg out of my lips and spoke for the first time in many months. It was as if with the peg I had opened a sluice and a torrent of words came out of my mouth, and my speaking lasted well into the morning sunshine. Never in my life had I spoken so much. I explained to the missionary that I wanted to have asylum in his hut, that the enforced silence of the peg and the lock was driving me crazy and that I needed a place where I could speak. All the time he was silent, stayed on his knees and kept his hands folded. While his eyes looked at me, I had the feeling that they looked through me. As I told him my entire life story I had the feeling that he was at the same time listening to a higher, more important voice than mine. Nothing seemed to deflect his constant attention to this inaudible voice and this radiant presence which I could not see. I told him that in return

8

for the asylum I would become his wife – at that he shook his head for a moment – without a bride price, since I was in the eyes of the community entirely worthless: a woman who could not be silenced even by the lock could not be entrusted with the up-bringing of children. I would – and I blushed violently – even accommodate myself to his strange sexual practices and do it with my hand for him, if he preferred that. But I felt that at that moment he was already no longer listening to me. His attention had fully returned to the inaudible voice, which to judge from his behaviour did seem to come from the piece of wood covered in various colours. But since he had neither thrown me out of his hut nor handed me over to the keeper of the speech I assumed that he had granted me asylum and had accepted my offer to be his wife.

So when, later that morning, the women of the village were sent to fetch me for punishment, I stepped out boldly into the entrance of his hut and told them that I was now the missionary's wife, that therefore the laws of the village no longer applied to me, that I could talk as long and as loud as I wanted to. There were horrified gasps of disbelief from all the women. Such a thing had never been experienced in the village before. But they returned to their men and explained how I had refused to come and be punished, as was demanded by our custom. The men sent the women away and held counsel for the rest of the day. As I could see from my hut large quantities of meat and beer were delivered to the hall of the sacred ancestors. Towards the evening they approached the hut of the missionary and the mayor de-manded to see him. The missionary, however, continued to listen to his voices, as if he had not heard their demand.

So it was again I who had to go to the entrance and speak for him. I stood there boldly, although my knees were quivering in fright, and spoke to them: The missionary does not deign to speak to such low creatures as you men. He is so far above you that he does not want to pollute his ears with your prattle.

The men made a noise like an angry swarm of bees. Never in history had a woman spoken to them like that.

Let us not listen to her crazy and obscene words, said one of the elders eventually. All the others nodded assent and continued to make angry noises. Let us just take her and punish her. Only the severest punishment is strong enough this time.

Stop, I said. The missionary is under the protection of his ancestors, and you know that you are not allowed to attack him. As I am now his wife, I am under the same protection. If you touch me, the protection of his ancestors will strike you dead.

There was a moment of shocked silence among the men. Then they all started to shout wildly, uttering curses, screaming that I should be abducted, that we should see whether our ancestors or the missionary's were stronger. But this time the elder and the mayor spoke to the assembled men and said that unfortunately they were unable to do anything as long as I was under the protection of the missionary and his ancestors. Gruesome stories about whole villages killed by the ancestors of missionaries who had been harmed in these places were common knowledge in our village, so most of the men accepted that nothing could be done to me.

As they left, grumbling, defeated, I was so elated by my victory that I shouted some of the obscenities which they recited at the solemn and ancient ritual of holy jokes, but they were so dejected that they did not even turn around to threaten me with the lock.

Once this was settled, I could move freely through the village, go wherever I wanted, but no man or woman wanted to talk to me. While I had completely cast off the peg, and considered myself a free woman not bound by the laws of the village, my freedom helped me nothing. Since nobody talked to me or even wanted to listen to me, my freedom was empty and meaningless. I soon found out that the situation in my own house was not any different. Although I could talk and talk as much as I wanted, I had the feeling that the missionary never listened to me. He was physically present in the hut, but his ears were somewhere else, and his mouth was eternally sealed.

I made an attempt to have sex with him, and one night when he was sleeping, using all the tricks which girls in our village are taught to please their husbands, I finally had him doing what man and wife do together in bed, and on that occasion found out that he was no different in his sexual preferences from any of our men. But the next morning he was hitting himself all over his naked body with the sharp nettles which grow in our village, until his body was one huge weal of nettle stings and covered with cuts bleeding profusely.

From then on he resisted any further advances, he always cast down his eyes so as not to see me in my beautiful nakedness, and he became even more fervently devoted to the voices which he heard. Everything I said was said as if into a vacuum, an empty room, was mere prattle and noise. Gradually I became violent, I hit him, I kicked him, I implored him to listen to me, but to no avail. The people of the village in the meantime were both shocked and constantly in peals of laughter about a man who could not control his woman, who even allowed her to hit him.

The whole situation was so outrageously wrong that a few young men, amongst them my future husband, decided to give me a lesson, and when I wandered through the village one day, abducted me and gave me a hiding. The mayor, who was afraid of the missionary's ancestors, came the next day to apologise to the silent missionary, though not to me. The band of young men was called to the mayor's house, led to the hut of unruliness and from there to the tribunal, where they were severely chastised.

The mayor then addressed all the men and the women of the village, declaring me mad. Only a woman who was completely deranged could have done the things I had done and could have spoken the way I had spoken. Since I was mad there was no shame in me, and thus no shame in my acts. None of the men should therefore feel himself shamed by my words or deeds. If the crazy missionary insisted on keeping me as his wife, using my hand for his sexual needs, then that was his affair, they as real men could only laugh about a man who was silent as a woman and who committed unspeakable acts with me. Missionaries, as we all knew, were crazy themselves but under the protection of very powerful ancestors. In short, they should simply continue to ignore me and not respond to whatever provocation.

I, in the meantime, was so frustrated with the unresponsive missionary that I ran around the village in the nude, talking and talking all the time, no longer caring if anybody listened, my hair in disarray and more and more dirty, fouling myself, drinking beer which I stole from kitchens momentarily unprotected. Nobody touched me any more. I became more and more like the mad woman the mayor had declared me to be.

One day I broke into the house of the ancestors, when the men were sharing their beer with the ruling spirits of the universe, the ancestors, in the solemn and ancient ritual of holy jokes about the curves of women's arses and breasts and the textures of their cunts. There was a shocked silence, because no woman had ever been allowed to enter this holy ground. My presence there, entirely unthinkable, defiled this holy place. I went and picked up a drinking vessel, filled it with beer, and drank, pouring some of it on the ground, greeting the ancestors, as if I were a man. None of the men had moved. It was as if my entrance had turned them all to stone.

Then I stood up and after uttering some of the customary obscenities I said: I am no longer the wife of the missionary. Herewith I end my marriage. That again had never happened in our village before. Of course, men are entirely at liberty to divorce a troublesome and talkative wife, in fact that is expected of them. They would be considered soft and under the spell of a woman if they tolerated such a wife. Often they only pretend that women are troublesome so as to be able to marry a younger wife.

But never before had a woman divorced a man, and only because the man was this strange and crazy missionary was the divorce accepted.

The divorce naturally brought me back under the guardianship of my father, and he, after consulting with the mayor, decided to bring me to a healer who lived a day's march away in the northern forests. My lips under lock and key, I was driven like a stray animal along the dusty roads through the maize fields and through the hot bush and the grass fields with cattle grazing on them to the edge of the dark forest. Following a narrow path amongst the gigantic trees down a ravine we finally arrived at a hut woven out of fern and grass at the edge of a small stream. There I was handed over to the healer, who asked that the lock be removed from my lips and then led me to a second, much smaller grass hut, where he indicated I had to wait in silence while he spoke to the men who had escorted me to this wild and inhospitable place.

After the men had gone the healer came to fetch me. He was a small wizened old man with grey hair and curiously agile eyes, and he was clad in wild animal skins and bearing a rod covered in coloured beads. For a long time we sat without talking. Then, as the shadows of the trees deepened, and after he had lit a fire and started to boil something on it, he began to talk to me, and his voice was soothing and spun a web of dreams around my troubled mind. It was the lure of this voice which eventually made me talk, tell him the one or other thing about my life, about my shameful compulsion to gossip. After many days of such talk I even confessed the blasphemous and hair-raising idea I had formed as a teenager that the peg is a torture which men have invented to humiliate women. He was always understanding and a good listener, so that in the end I even related the horrifying story of my marriage to the missionary and my desecration of the hut of the ancestors. I could see that he paled for a moment at such outrageous behaviour, which must have been unheard-of even to someone who had dealt with many crazy and deranged women in his life, but he quickly gained control over himself again, and listened to the story as if it were a common and every-day occurrence that a woman should talk back to men who had come to fetch her for punishment.

After three months of staying with the healer, and after my mouth had been purged of its dirty gossip several times with a concoction made of very bitter roots, the healer declared me healed, and sent me back to the village.

When I arrived there, I met again the group of young men who had beaten me up while I was married to the missionary. One of them stepped forward and said to me: Although you are an incur-able gossip, I have decided to make you my wife, and your father has agreed to give you to me without a bride price. I have made a wager with my comrades here that I will be the one to cure you of your habit of gossiping.

There was nothing I could do, and I followed my husband to his hut. It took only two days before my lips were back in the lock, because the habit of talking daily to the healer had pam-pered my desire to gossip, and I was not used any more not to say what came into my mind whenever it came into my mind. On this occasion I asked one of my girlhood friends what had happened to the missionary, whose hut I saw stood empty. My friend con-fided to me in agitated whispers that one day while I was at the healer's, this strange man the missionary had burned down the hall of the ancestors, had stood before the burning house and spoken for the first time since he came to the village, saying that they must abandon their evil customs and embrace a thing which he called Jesus. The men, who were very angry, shouted at him that never would they be converted to his strange sexual prac-tices, that they were quite content to embrace their wives and would never sink as low as to embrace a thing like Jesus. Since they were not allowed to touch the missionary, the men sent a delegation to the town, which is several days away, and complained there that the missionary had gone crazy and would they please fetch him. A few days after they returned, three white men in strange clothes came and took him away.

Despite the wager my husband had made, he did not succeed in silencing me, and even after we had had several children together, I had to be put under lock again and again. When he had to pay out his age-mates on the wager, he became really furious, and one night he dragged me down to near the brook just outside our village where the overhanging trees trail their branches in the streaming water. There he took out a huge butcher's knife and said: Since I have not been able to silence you by any other means, I am now going to cut your throat.

For the first time in my life I was speechless. My lips quivered but did not make a sound. I fell on my knees and lifted my hands and implored him to spare me with that gesture. But I was unable to utter a single word.

From that moment on I became as silent as the missionary, my first husband. I never spoke again. But three weeks later I poisoned my husband with a plant which I had learnt how to cook at the healer's hut. He died in terrible cramps, shouting abuse at me and my cooking. Nobody ever found out that I had killed him, and since I could no longer speak, I could not betray myself by idle talk.

The kaffir who read books

AROUND HERE THERE ARE NOT all that many people who
read. Mind you, there are quite a lot who *can* read, they
have been to school and all that, but I mean read for pleasure.
Those who have been to school regard reading as something you
do to pass the exam, and they firmly believe that you should decidedly not inflict that kind of pain on yourself unless you really have to. Anyway, if you did want to indulge in that perverse,
masochistic kind of pain, where would you get anything to read,
except perhaps an old newspaper or a glossy women's magazine
which some white madam had thrown into the trashcan. Books
being as expensive as they are, the cheapest cost as much as
three days' salary, and most people here certainly have better
things to do with their hard-earned cash than to buy books. And
as for libraries: well, however hard you look, you will not find
any libraries in this place. Because, see, blacks don't read, or so
they say.

So everybody agreed that Mbulelo was quite strange, and
probably a little mad: whenever the weather was bearable, he
would sit in front of his wooden shack on a little bench he had
made himself, one of his tattered books in his hand, reading
intently. His eyes were the only things which moved from side to

side, up and down, occasionally he would mumble something, sometimes he would laugh, when nobody around could find anything ridiculous in the surroundings, sometimes he would be sad even if it was the most wonderful sunny April day, with the children playing their noisy games and everybody going about happily.

Those who knew Mbulelo before he could read said that he never really went to school and learned to read and write at all. He learned to read as an adult, when his son Tom went to school, and he asked Tom to teach him the rudiments of reading. Now imagine this: an adult, grown man, learning from an eight-year-old. We were all laughing, of course. Anyway, we all agreed, adults can no longer learn the stuff they teach you at school. That kind of stuff you can only learn at school, where the teachers beat it into you, until your stubborn brain capitulates and absorbs it long enough for you to be able to pass the exam. Learning, we all knew, only occurred if you used a long stick, and you can't, after all, cane an adult.

The funny thing was, he proved us all wrong. It took him three years to go through Tom's graded readers in the evenings in the light of a petroleum lamp, and on Sundays, then he seemed to have got the hang of it, because he got two old children's books from the white madam where he worked as a gardener on Saturdays, for his son, as he said, but in reality for himself as well. When the two of them had been through the children's books he looked out for other reading material. There was, of course, the occasional discarded newspaper he would pick up, but he did not really like to read the papers – unlike John, the newspaperboy, who regularly reads the paper while he sits on the kerb of the traffic island, waiting for drivers to stop and hail him with outstretched arm. No, he wanted books, real books. Now, as I said before, books were way too expensive for all of us. Besides, when he once went into a bookshop, he was so overawed by the amount of books that he had no idea which ones to spend the twenty rand on that he had saved up over the last six months. After he had stared at the unbelievable riches stacked on the shelves and on display tables for a few minutes, one of the salesladies approached, saying:

And what do you want, *boy*?

He was completely flustered and stammered that he wanted to buy a book.

Oh, so you are a white educated kaffir, are you? she screamed, laughing. Oh, you can read. A book, she laughed, he wants a book. Sure, so what about some Shakespeare?

That was the ultimate in white wit. Shakespeare to her must have been the summit of white culture, something which no *native* would ever be able to understand, because even she, the saleslady in a bookshop, could not understand Shakespeare when she was required to read *Hamlet* for matric.

Is it a good book, asked Mbulelo, this Shakespeare?

This of course brought forth more hoots of laughter from the saleslady. He wanted to buy a book, and had not even heard of Shakespeare. And she shouted to the cashier:

This black *gentleman* wants to read Shakespeare! Imagine. Shakespeare!

As it turned out, they did not have any Shakespeare in the shop, because Shakespeare is not much in demand even in white suburbs, and Mbulelo grabbed his twenty rand and left the shop, followed by hysterical peals of laughter. That was the last time he entered a bookshop, because soon afterwards he found a much cheaper source of books, affordable even for him, and in a much less threatening atmosphere. Working as a gardener for one of the churches in the southern suburbs, he was required to help with the annual church bazaar. And there among the cookie stands, and the koeksister stands, the stands with white elephants and "antique" crockery, between the braaivleis stand and the school-uniform stand he found a table full of books, the price uniformly five or ten cents. Now ten cents then was a lot of money, but he could scrape that together every few weeks, and so he searched for notices saying: church bazaar or school bazaar, and in this way started to build up his library. There were old schoolbooks – he even found a tattered copy of Shakespeare's *Macbeth* there, complete with annotations which explained the antiquated words he could not understand at first – there were travel books, there were novels, poetry anthologies and history books.

For many years he collected second-hand books, and he even built himself a bookrack in the shack where there was hardly enough place to sit down or to sleep anyway, made of wooden planks and bricks which he picked up wherever he found them. At first it was very hard going: the English in which these books were written was mostly far beyond his understanding, and even Tom, who went to school, could not explain what many of the words meant. But somewhere he found an old *English-Kaffir Dictionary* which translated some of the unfamiliar words into words he knew, and after some time of faithfully looking up every word he did not understand, he began to grasp the meaning of unfamiliar words from their context. From that moment on the speed of his reading became faster and faster. He even found that with the help of the glossary and the explanatory notes he could read Shakespeare, who at first had seemed to write totally unintelligible gibberish, and whom he now enjoyed thoroughly. Foul whisperings are abroad, he read out to his son, unnatural deeds do breed unnatural troubles: infected minds to their deaf pillows will discharge their secrets.

That sounds like a good description of the South African situation, said Tom.

Well, Shakespeare is for everyone, said Mbulelo.

Among the discarded bestsellers from England and America he once picked up a novel by an African writer, the orange cover bleached, the author's photograph cut by white creases, but it was a recognizably African face in its dignity and sadness.

Hey, he said to Tom, when he came home: Look what I picked

up today at the Bishop's school bazaar. And he held out the tattered copy of his book, the pages coming loose from the spine.

Ngugi wa Thiong'o, Tom deciphered, giving the African name an English pronunciation. What a strange name.

An African writer, shouted Mbulelo. You know, I never believed that there were Africans who wrote books.

Petals of Blood, read Tom. Now what does that mean? *Petals of Blood*? Must be a crime novel!

For the next few days father and son read this novel to each other whenever there was a free moment in their lives, and they followed the story of Munira, Wanja, Karega and Abdulla with bated breath. At first it really looked like a thriller with three guys murdered, and the suspects picked up by the police, a kind of jigsaw puzzle, where you attempted to guess who the murderer was, before the author told you. But then they understood that the novel was really about the destruction of village life and that things in Kenya were not so different from things in South Africa, when the writer described how all the young men and women moved away from the village to the big town after the glittering metal and how the village became a place of old women who looked after their grandchildren dropped there by their mothers working in town. They read how a once thriving community not afraid to live on the sweat of their hands, started its decline and depopulation, and how in turn it became the property of fat-stomach developers who exploited its position on the Trans-Africa road. They read about Dedan Kimathi and the battle against the English and the betrayal of the people by those who became its leaders after the war, they read about the drought and the poverty and the hunger of the people, about their long journey to the big town and their attempt to obtain help from the elected leaders of the people, they read how the people of Ilmorog were cheated out of their land by their black brothers who had become vultures of the people, who had now become the directors of multinational companies, and how these same directors who had betrayed the people all along burned to death in the house of Wanja. And while they found Kenya in the school atlas, somewhere far away in East Africa, what happened in the novel sounded very like their own experience.

This was the time of the student unrest, a state of emergency had been declared, and Mbulelo was much worried about the education of his son. As the boycotts grew longer, the school became more like a wartime ruin every day, the books were burned, tables splintered, chairs were used as barricades, and the windows smashed by flying stones and police bullets. Mbulelo had long arguments with Tom who was now fourteen about the necessity of education, and he countered all of the boy's arguments about the necessity of bringing down the apartheid regime first before they could get a decent education with his standard argument that he was obviously merely too lazy or too stupid to benefit from education, and anyway apartheid may be around for some time to come, whereas if he did not make it at school he would not get another chance. To make up at least partially for what he saw as the loss of a singular opportunity, he made Tom read to him his history and physics books, explain to him mathematics and poetry, recite geography and grammar.

Of course, Tom tried to escape this unofficial school whenever he could to be with his comrades, and one day he simply did not return from one of his exploits. Later that evening when it was dark, a girl of Tom's age came around to the house to say that he had been detained at school.

At that time there was talk that the squatter community where Mbulelo lived was to be moved to Khayelitsha. Mbulelo did not take this all too seriously at first, because there had been various attempts in the past he could remember, where the government had tried to "clean up" the squatter camps, but since they had won a legal battle in the Supreme Court in 1976 entitling them to stay, there had been no serious attempt to move them. The daily hassles and harassment continued all the time, of course, and if you did not have a valid pass, and sometimes even if you had one, you very often enjoyed a free ride to the Transkei, although you had to pay the fare to come back, clandestinely. At that time there were almost daily police raids to catch "illegal" squatters. There were fights between the people, people were killed, cars set alight, windows broken, telephone wires cut. As Mbulelo did not like the way the squatter leader Ngxobongwana handled the situation, he moved his shack to a new site, which was called KTC, and later "New Crossroads". It was there that the police were particularly heavy-handed, but since his pass was in order, and since he had regular employment, for the moment he succeeded in holding on to his shack.

When one community councillor, who came to survey the shacks at Crossroads accompanied by two policemen, told him that all this squatting was against the laws of the country, and that they had all broken the law, Mbulelo said quietly: These laws are crazy. I am sure that God does not agree with these laws of the white man. A man has to live somewhere, and since there are no houses for us, we live here, and we have been living here for many years.

Despite the constant harassment Mbulelo was much more worried about his son than his shack, as for more than three months he did not hear anything from him, although an occasional night visitor in Tom's age group would tell him that while he had been tortured in jail he seemed to be in good health again, and there was nothing to worry about. Mbulelo, who knew how such messages were smuggled out of jail, resigned himself to waiting. Finally he received his first letter from Tom himself, who assured him that he was fine.

Mbulelo did not belong either to the comrades of the UDF or to the new group which had formed in Crossroads, the witdoeke, the thugs who were supporting the squatter leader Ngxobongwana, and at first he did not understand why two black groups should attack each other, tear down each other's shacks and burn them, and kill each other. But when the people living in KTC refused to move to Khayelitsha – "Asiyi eKhayelitsha!" they chanted – he joined them in their protests, and when he was asked to help with the teaching in the school which the squatters had built in New Crossroads, he did so whenever he had some free time.

At times the police would come with their hippos and mellow yellows and arrest people and cart them away to Bishop Lavis, Pollsmoor and Mitchells Plain. There were protests and then the police would shoot with rubber bullets and teargas. The homes of some of the people who had been arrested were burned at night by unknown people. When some comrades threw a hand grenade into the house of one of the leaders of "the fathers", the leader swore revenge:

We cannot leave our children to play with us, we are seriously injured already. The children are very disrespectful to the fathers. What we need is more discipline in the townships. Unless the *maqabane* cool down, the people of Old Crossroads will hunt them down and beat them again. The *maqabane* have to stop making petrol bombs and holding kangaroo courts. We will not allow them to punish and beat their own people.

Mbubelo tended to agree with that. He did not like all this fighting and chaos.

But as his son was a well-known leader of the "children", his house even at that time was, unknown to him, on the hitlist of the "fathers". They wanted to punish anybody who had helped the "comrades" or who was connected with them. So one night he was woken up by the sound of gunshots. Voices screaming in terror mingled with the sound of shots striking his corrugated-iron roof. His door was kicked in, several policemen burst in, and roughly pulled Mbulelo outside. They pointed their guns at him and asked him where his son had hidden his weapons and the landmines. Mbulelo told them that he knew nothing about this. They hit him and dragged him away to a mellow yellow. As he turned he saw a group of witdoeke pouring petrol over the wooden planks of his house and putting it to fire.

When Mbulelo was released the next morning, he returned to KTC. He found his house totally burned down. Many other houses had been burned. Nothing which belonged to him remained except for a few pans and pots, blackened by soot. He picked up the remnants of his belongings, and together with a friend walked over to Portland Cement, where, after he had phoned his employer, over the next few days he built another, even smaller shack. He bought a new suit and a new working outfit fairly cheaply from a friend who peddled stolen goods in the squatter camp. Then he went back to work.

One Saturday evening, just after he had come back from work, he heard a few shots. As he cautiously looked outside, he saw two white soldiers setting the hut of his neighbour on fire. A bit further on he saw a man with the white headband of the witdoeke throw a burning tyre on to the roof of a house which caught fire immediately. Mbulelo took his clothes and whatever else he could carry and moved away through the night from the danger zone into the Port Jackson bushes. He did not get much sleep that night. There was constant gunfire throughout the night, the sounds of heavy motor vehicles churning up the dust and the sand of the squatter camp, and the flickering light of flames everywhere. By the time the sun came up the whole of Portland Cement was ablaze.

During the day Mbulelo managed to rummage through the ruins of his second shack and retrieve the few possessions which had not been burned to ashes. That afternoon he joined those who moved to Site C because he wanted to have some peace and quiet, and because it was clear to him that Crossroads would remain a battlefield until the last opponents of the move were either killed or in jail.

Mbulelo did not see his son for more than fifteen months. By the time he was released from police custody, their house had already been destroyed and Mbulelo had built a new one, and that had also been destroyed, and now Mbulelo lived in a tent in Site C in Khayelitsha. Many others were detained during this period, and many more were killed. When Tom did come home, he was taciturn and spent whole days sitting in the tent or lying on the mattress not sleeping but not really awake either.

Until one day he said: But father, where are all your books?

Ah, Mbulelo said, you know they have all been burned in Crossroads. And I don't have the money or the heart to buy books any more. I was foolish enough to believe that one should become educated and being educated one would escape from these squatter camps. But to them you remain the kaffir, no matter what. Worse, you are a kaffir who reads books, and since most of them don't read themselves, they feel threatened. They say they are civilised, but they only have a white skin. And they know it, and they fear us being better than them.

Mbulelo sighed and walked out of the tent.

The next day Tom walked all the way to Observatory – he had no money for the bus – and searched for an address. Finally he found the house he was looking for. But when he rang nobody opened. So he sat on the stairs in front of the door for three and a half hours until a young man of about twenty-five came up the street.

Tom! the young man shouted, are you out? Come in, come in, and have a beer.

They sat down in the little room, Walter opened two beers, and they talked about the time they had spent together in the struggle, and what had happened to them since Tom was detained, and it was beginning to get dark by the time Tom came out with his request.

You know my father was a great collector of books. Reading was his greatest pleasure since I taught him as an eight-year-old kid. Well, when they destroyed Crossroads all his books went up in flames. He hasn't been reading since. Nor have I, except for the Bible in jail.

He hesitated.

Well, what I came to ask is, can you lend us a few books?

Sure, said Walter, as long as they do find their way back here. What do you want to read in particular?

You wouldn't have any Ngugi wa Thiong'o, would you?

Sure, I have got everything he has ever published – well, nearly. Why don't you try *Matigari*? I loved that!

If it doesn't get burned again, I will bring it back as soon as we have read it, said Tom with a smile.

So late that evening Tom went home with a copy of *Matigari* under his arm.

The next day was a Sunday, and they settled in the shade of the tent, and the father opened the book and began to read to his son:

He held an AK 47 in his right hand. His left hand was raised to shield his face while he looked across the river, as he had often done over many years, across many hills and valleys, in the four corners of the globe.

Waiting for Mandela

ONE OF THE THINGS WHICH you don't do if you live off your wits is move in a straight line, ever. Much too easy to be caught and much too conspicuous. I mean, I was told over and over again by my mother to think straight. But thinking straight gets you nowhere. Thinking straight makes it easy for the other guy to catch up with you, because he can guess what you are thinking. All those straight guys, you just need to watch them twice, listen to them carefully, and you will know what they are going to say or do the third time, and the fourth time, and so it is easy to second-guess them. Now, if you want to survive in this game, you have to think like a swarm of sparrows. You get too near where they are taking the pickings and they explode in a maze of zigzags. Try and catch one, even with a gun and bird-shot. No way! I know all that. So I really have no excuse at all. Just plain, fokken stupidity. That's all.

Thinking straight to the loot, that was my mistake! After all, I should have known that such a big meeting meant lots of police. When we came at three there were already thousands and thousands of people. One large group was toyi-toying around that funny king statue with its shiny bald head and its funny night-gown in the middle of the Parade, they had given him a big cloth over his mouth and nose so he looked like *iqabane* fighting the police, and they had a black, green and yellow flag up there, and there were about a dozen of them clinging to the statue. And there were dozens of these flags all over the place. Johnny who reads second-hand newspapers out of dustbins told me that these were the flags of the African National Congress, and then he pointed to the red flags of the Communists. I thought the Communists were banned like in South Africa, and that they were really bad guys, such as not even a criminal would like to shake their hands, but Johnny said they had been unbanned last week. So maybe there is hope for us petty criminals. The Parade was crammed full of people by three, so you hardly could move. There were even people on the walls of the fort and on the parking garage near Strand Street. At first the police were inconspicuous in the side streets. And Johnny said they would not want to interfere with such a big crowd. Imagine a hundred thousand, two hundred thousand or more starting to stampede. What a riot.

When Johnny came around on Saturday evening with a soiled newspaper he had picked up in a waste-paper basket next to the station, he was all excited like: Look here, they are going to let Mandela out of prison. It says here.

Now, I can't read, so I take his word for it. Anyway, what's it got to do with me?

He says: There's going to be a big meeting at the Parade, and he is going to speak there at three.

So, I say, what's that to get all excited like? Since when are you interested in fokken politics.

Ag, man, he says, it's just real cool blue like, that they let him go after all these years. I mean, he is a great guy. I mean he is for us blacks getting equality.

I still don't get it, man. And what does this equality mean, anyway?

Man, you're stupid. It means we are going to be like these whites, have houses and swimming pools and TVs and we're going to have a say in things. This guy has been fighting for us blacks for years, and they put him in jail for 28 years, so he is really one of us. We ought to make him an honorary member of the Mongrels.

If you ask me, I'm thinking, my view is that a guy who gets caught by the police and put into prison for 28 years wouldn't even make a good honorary member of the Mongrels, whatever that *honorary* may mean. But nobody asks me so I don't tell Johnny.

Now, I say, Johnny, you're really naive. That guy is a politician. Politicians land up in jail, when they fight each other. But they are never fighting for us. I mean, if this guy ever makes it to prime minister or president, do you really believe he will be on our side? Like shit, he will. If he catches you, he is going to put you in jail just like the present guy or the past guy. In fact he won't even know you are in jail, he is too busy counting the big money and riding in his shiny Mercedes and chaffing the ladies.

I'm still for him, he says, because he is against them. After all, he was in jail like me. And man, was he a legend. Everyone told these stories, how he was sort of uppity against these warders, until they stopped being bloody. Anyway, I'm going to go tomorrow. I want to see this.

I wasn't convinced, but then I thought, well, maybe, when there is a big crowd and they are all squeezed in so that nobody can move, that is a good place to put your hands into the pockets of other people. And maybe there is some rioting at the edges, as there often is, with youngsters getting impatient with this here freedom taking so long to come, and taking a stone in their hand to hasten the advent of the freedom by a few minutes. In a situation like this there is a great likelihood of windows getting broken and of sort of valuable things getting lost which look so appealing behind washed shop window panes. So I said, what the hell, I mean a guy has to live and a big political rally is as good as a railway concourse, if not better.

29

The newspapers had said that people should be at the Parade at two, so reckoning that people usually come late to meetings like this we took the train at half past two and arrived at three at the station. The town was very quiet sort of, hardly anybody in sight except these groups of people in green, gold and black T-shirts or with the face of this Mandela guy printed on them or with a shield and a spear like. They all looked sort of excited and happy, and I thought that that was the right kind of mood for me, they would hardly notice my fingers in their pockets with all that happiness in their faces.

It was bloody hot by the time we walked across Strand Street and saw the huge crowd. I mean it was so hot your shoes melted through the tarmac. Their faces were all turned towards the city hall, that clumsy building of reddish-grey sandstone with its black columns at the balcony and its funny windows with round tops. There was another of those big green, yellow and black flags hanging from a balcony, and a guy who was standing behind a microphone and talking to the people, but obviously they did not want to listen to him. He told them to move back and listen to the marshalls, but it did not seem that they were much impressed by this kind of talk.

At the back of the crowd it was fairly easy to move, although even here people stood densely packed. As we moved across the Parade, the squeeze was becoming more noticeable, and often we were not able to move at all. It was at this point that I stood behind an Indian guy and his lady in a sari, and I immediately smelled the pocket money which was waiting for me. And, just as there was some pushing starting around us with people shouting "Amandla" and "Ngawethu", my fingers made it into his jacket from behind and found it. It was a delicate operation, and of course I did not make the mistake of looking at my loot, but let it quietly disappear into my right trouser pocket and started to drift towards the right with no apparent haste but yet steadily and with success.

It was at that moment that I must have lost Johnny. I was in a group of young people, blacks and coloureds, and a few whites, students, if you ask me. They were getting impatient like. Now that is always the best time. They're always so impatient to get where they want to get, so they try to move in a straight line, because they are in a hurry, and of course they fuck it all up. They haven't learned that in order to get anywhere and to get away with it, you must move in crooked lines. They think they are intelligent because they've gone to school and learned to read and all that, but they are fokken stupid, nevertheless. You must flow with the crowd, to be inconspicuous, and use their energy to get where you want to get. And I got there sooner or later, sooner than all of them.

The squeeze was getting worse and worse. Everybody was pushing forward towards the green, black and gold balcony, although there was nothing to see at all at this moment, the microphone deserted, the black and white dignitaries in urgent conversation in the dark shadows behind some curtains. But I got to the very heart of the thing. In front of me was a line of people who desperately shouted to the crowd to keep behind the barriers, and who had formed a human chain to push back the impatient followers of the man who was supposed to be here already, but who was nowhere to be seen. To my right there was what appeared to be a car trying to force its way through the crowd, to my left a huge lorry with a crane was completely covered by human bodies clinging to their vantage point. Two guys were even parking on top of a no-stopping sign waving that black, green and yellow flag of theirs.

This very big white guy, who towered above the others like Mount Kilimanjaro, was taking a picture just as I took the money out of the guy's pocket right in the first line behind the marshalls. I don't think my hand will be on the photo, although my face will be there, as my hand was all covered up by the many bodies. But I thought I better move sideways and out of the immediate vicinity before the guy notices that the leaves have fallen. While I drifted through the crowd, women were fainting because it was so hot and because of the pressure of the crowd. Some had to be lifted over the heads of the crowd to get them out, because the crowd could not even open up a way for the first-aid guys to get through. That is how impenetrable that crowd was. It took me half an hour of thinking sideways before I came near the edge of the crowd, and I can tell you I wasn't lazy all that time. My pockets were bulging. If I had been sensible, I would have gone home then and there, but I was nosy and I moved round the back of the city hall to the other side of the crowd. A lot of people were walking to and from the crowd by now, the ones who came back had cooldrinks and hamburgers or hotdogs in their hands. It was bloody hot, the tar of the streets was beginning to boil, and I felt thirsty, so I asked one of the guys where they get this refreshment, and they showed me the way to the only shop in the surroundings which was open, and sure enough there was a huge queue in front of the shop and it took me nearly half an hour to get even near to the door. I should have taken the train home and got a real drink there. So when I came to the door, the people in front were shouting and complaining, and it seemed that there was no more cooldrinks or stuff. I was quite pissed off, you know, having stood there for half an hour and now nothing.

So I took a detour round the Parade trying to get to the station. As I went along I saw a few guys were standing in front of a broken shop window and stuffing shirts and trousers under their T-shirts. That kind of thing is not for me, as I reckon that this bulky kind of stuff is much more easily seen than gold chains and twenty-rand notes in my pocket. So I moved on quickly and sure enough, as I turn the corner there is this troop of soldiers in helmets and plastic visors before their faces and guns at the ready marching down the street in single file. So I have a feeling that the scene is getting too hot for the likes of me and move towards the station a bit faster. There is a bit of a quiet stretch ahead of me, and just as a precaution I take out the three wallets I had nabbed, and open them. I just take the money because all these cards are just a nuisance, you just get into trouble with them, and it seems there are about two hundred and fifty rand altogether, apart from the few ten- and twenty-rand notes which I fished out of pockets. Then I throw the wallets into the next waste-paper basket. With all the fuss about perhaps it would be a good idea to get rid of the gold chains as well. I mean I can explain the notes, they are my hard-earned weekly salary, but it is a bit awkward to explain ladies' gold chains in your pocket. So I put them round my neck under my shirt. I mean a man is entitled to wear a gold chain, isn't he? These days the guys are even wearing earrings and diamonds in their noses.

When I turned round the corner that was when the real action started. There was a large unruly mob running around and shouting. A big black guy with his face covered under a black, green and gold shawl threw a bottle into the shopfront window, other bottles followed, the window shattered, glass splinters flew all over the place. Out of the crowd came two guys with black, green and gold bandages round their arm and shouted: Comrades, please, stop this. But they were shoved aside by the young people. The next moment some of them were in the display window and threw out trousers, shirts, jackets, the lot. I snatched a trouser and raced off to the left, where between two parked cars I got rid of my old torn trouser and put on the brand new one, not forgetting to shift the money from the old trouser to the new, of course.

By the time I came back, they had smashed the window of a shoe store, and the marshalls were still trying to stop the looters. One big guy stood in the middle of the display window, awkwardly balancing on the little pedestals, and threw out shoes by the handful. People laughed, screamed, shouted, and jostled to catch the loot, but mostly a guy would catch one shoe and then look for the other of the pair and not find it, because somebody else had already caught it. It was then that the police arrived and started shooting immediately. Many people dived for cover behind the low walls and kerbs next to the road or just flopped down on the street. As we ran away, a young guy next to me fell to the road and remained lying there. But in such a situation it is everyone for himself and the devil take the hindmost. When I reached the entrance of the station, I felt a sharp pain on my leg, and stumbled. To my horror I saw blood streaming down from my calf. Looking around I saw this huge policeman storm down on me and before I could get up again, he hit me over the head with his truncheon.

When I regained consciousness, my hands were handcuffed. At that very moment an indescribable roar went up: there was shouting of "Amandla", chants of "Viva! Viva!" and near hysterical screaming from the crowds on the Parade. The policeman who had hit me, picked me up and made me walk towards the police van.

He is here now, they all shouting like mad, one of the policemen said.

Then there came his voice over the loudspeakers. I knew it was him immediately, although I had never heard his voice before. With quiet authority which immediately stopped the wild shouting of vivas and amandlas he began: I extend special greetings to the people of Cape Town, the city which has been my home for three decades. Your mass marches and other forms of struggle have served as a constant source of strength to all political prisoners.

The policeman who stood next to the van said to the one who pushed me: Do you understand this? I mean this Mandela guy. We go to all the trouble to catch them, and then the politicians let them loose again.

That's politics for you, said my policeman.

Friends, comrades and fellow South Africans, Mandela's voice filled the space. I greet you all in the name of peace, democracy and freedom for all. I stand here before you not as prophet, but as a humble servant of you, the people.

Hey, kaffir, get into the van, shouted my policeman.

But even inside the van I could hear him: Your tireless and heroic sacrifices have made it possible for me to be here today. I therefore place the remaining years of my life in your hands.

Then two others brought a guy whose face was all cut up, the blood streaming down into his shirt. They threw him into the back, where he lay as if dead. I was scared, I can tell you. I was shit scared. They brought another six guys, who all looked a little dazed. They probably had had the sjambok treatment like me.

Mandela's voice continued: Today the majority of South Africans, black and white, recognise that apartheid has no future. It has to be ended by our own decisive mass action in order to build peace and security.

Bloody fokken communist, mumbled one of the policemen. Fokken kaffir agitator! Stupid baboon! Bloody insane terrorist!

I fokken well don't know what has come over fokken De Klerk, said another. I mean this is fokken trouble, and it is us who will fokken well have to handle it. My fokken God!

When we drove off, over the noise of the engine, I still heard him, and his voice followed us: The apartheid destruction on our subcontinent is incalculable. The fabric of family life of millions of our people has been shattered. Millions are homeless and unemployed, our economy lies in ruins and our people are embroiled in political strife.

He's got a point there, I thought, as we rounded the corner into Adderley Street. I've been unemployed since I was six, and homeless too, and hungry most of the time.

As we were driving, I threw the money and the two gold chains out through the bars on to the road and they floated off in the wind. I thought it would not be a good idea to arrive at the police station with all that cash in my pocket and two gold chains around my neck. Especially since I had no known means of support as they call it in court, which means I have not done a stroke of work since I was six.

So what did you do that for? asked one of the guys.

I just looked at him: What?

Throwing good money out of the window.

Did you see me do anything? I asked him threateningly.

No, brother, I seen nothing, he laughed.

OK, that's my boy.

At the police station they had the TV on. Mandela's voice reached me while we were pushed into the cells: We have waited too long for our freedom. We can no longer wait. Now is the time to intensify the struggle on all fronts. To relax our efforts now would be a mistake which generations to come will not forgive. The sight of freedom looming on the horizon should encourage us to redouble our efforts. It is only through disciplined mass action that our victory can be assured.

I couldn't hear the end of his speech, because then the door to the cells was slammed and his voice faded. After that I had a lot of time to think about my stupidity. All this loot I had to throw out of the van's window, it really grieves me, man, my heart aches. And they will probably get me for the trousers anyway. So six months in the cooler. I mean I know one of the things which you don't do if you live off your wits is move in a straight line, ever. I know it, and yet I let myself be caught making straight for the loot and then straight for the escape route instead of scattering when I got the first smell of the fuzz. I know that if you want to survive in this game, you have to think like a swarm of Cape Town city sparrows.

You have to explode in a maze of zigzags. Try and catch one, even with a gun. No way! I know all that. So I really have no excuse at all. Just plain, fokken stupidity. That's all.

Not born of a father or mother

IT IS DIFFICULT TO PIN down the exact moment when the new slogan was first heard and then accepted by all the Young Lions of the township. It seemed to have sprung out of the earth, just as it proclaimed that the Young Lions were without father or mother, without ancestors, that they just *were*. The Young Lions are born of the struggle, it said, and was understood to mean that, since the parent generation had not succeeded in throwing off the yoke of the oppressor, had indeed allowed itself to be subjugated most shamefully, it simply did not count, need not be counted in the genealogy of the struggle, and could not even be honoured for having brought forth the young generation biologically. The Young Lions thus created an image of themselves as having sprung forth out of the stony ground of the townships, fully armed with Molotov cocktails and rocks, assegais and pistols, AK 47s and limpet mines.

Some had parted from the safety of their homes with regret, but, knowing the necessity of cutting the ties which they experienced as hindering shackles, had done so swiftly and neatly; others had translated their juvenile revolt against the older generation into a morally superior stance, and revelled in the violent conflict with parents and teachers, which at last allowed them to

37

express openly, and with the communal support of their entire generation, what they had previously experienced only as the usual struggle between parents and children; others again, while openly adhering to this new-found independence of the young from their elders, never cut the ties with their parents completely, but visited them furtively whenever possible, and only became sheepishly scornful of the older generation when the presence of their comrades demanded this.

Xola, one of the young leaders, whose father worked as a "boy" at a garage in Observatory, and whose mother was a live-in maid in Kenilworth, was particularly harsh in his condemnation of the passivity of the older generation. He had left his home, a small box of a house with only two rooms, and was constantly on the run from the police, after he had been identified by a spy as one of the most important leaders of the youth. During his period of hiding in the underground, while he moved from house to house, and never stayed longer at any one place than a single night, his father was killed in an accident, as he crossed the Main Road in Observatory to walk to the bus station in the evening. The news of his father's death reached Xola many days later, as nobody knew where he was staying at that time, and quite by accident. One of the fellow-workers of his father saw him, as he alighted from the late-evening bus, and asked him why he had not at least come home for the burial of his father.

Xola did not react outwardly in any way to the news of his father's death, except to swallow hard a few times. It was impossible even to go home and mourn with his mother, as that would have meant certain arrest, but he at least managed to smuggle a letter to her that same night, telling her that he was safe and expressing his sorrow at the death of his father. Towards his comrades, however, he expressed no sorrow and no regret. If anything he became even harsher in his condemnation of the older generation, which allowed itself to be killed for nothing in the service of the white baas.

A few weeks later the news reached Xola that his mother had been shot by a group of young policemen, who were terrorising the neighbourhood, as she alighted from the bus on a Sunday afternoon, her only time off from her job. This time the news reached Xola within minutes, as he was hiding in a house close to the scene of the senseless massacre. For the first time Xola broke down completely, wanting to storm out of his safe house and kill the policemen then and there. Three strong comrades could hardly hold him back from his foolish undertaking. He wept openly for many hours, no longer caring whether his comrades approved or not. They also had to restrain him and watch over him on the following Sunday, when his mother was buried by the entire community. But not even the attendance of a crowd of several hundred mourners, all expressing the outrage of the township dwellers over this senseless killing, would have been security enough for him to attend the funeral. The graveyard was encircled by police and soldiers in armoured vehicles, and there was little chance of entering and leaving it without being recognised.

For the next few weeks he was even unable to visit her grave, as there were reports of the police having staked out the cemetery constantly, obviously in the hope of catching him if he went there. When they gave up, his visit to the graveyard was a major logistical undertaking, with watchers all over the place. Xola was lucky, the cemetery was deserted, he spent some time at the grave of his mother and finally left with his comrades for another hiding place in Nyanga East.

While constantly on the look-out for the police and police spies, Xola and his small group moved through the backyards of the townships, jumping over fences, sneaking into ill-lit kitchens for a scanty meal, recruiting other youngsters to join them in the struggle, founding cells of resistance in the sprawling townships and shack-dwellers' locations all over the Cape Flats. His group of hardened warriors appeared wherever the youth was involved in fights with the police, throwing stones and "guava juices", and disappearing as mysteriously as they had come. In this way the myth of the warriors who sprang from the earth fully armed, but without parents, the avengers of the township and the precursors of freedom, spread through all the townships of the Cape Flats. From time to time, some members of the cell were caught by the police, some, the victims of their own daring, when they did not retreat fast enough from the lines of advancing policemen; the one or the other betrayed by a shebeen owner angry at the Christmas boycott of alcohol imposed by the Young Lions or by a taxi driver who made some extra money selling information to Lieutenant Jan van Dyck at the Guguletu police station.

Constantly on the move, hidden by friendly supporters, often at considerable risk to themselves, the group seemed to dissolve into the bleak landscape of the township in such a way that the police, despite their efforts, were unable to predict where they would hit next or where they would spend the next night.

Then came the news that Xola's two young sisters, Pumla and Nonkululeko, had been raped by a gang, the A-Team, named after an American TV serial, who ruled most of the sprawling squatter camps around Crossroads. Xola, blinded by rage, met his sisters two nights later in the shack of one of the leaders of the squatter community near the airport, where the two young women had been given shelter. They were terrified to go back to their own shack, which they had built with the help of a few of Xola's comrades after the death of their parents and the loss of their house. Xola embraced his two sisters, who were crying when they saw him. With stern and unmoving face, Xola listened to the description of the men involved in the outrage. Late that night Xola disappeared into the warren of shacks, and was not heard of for a few weeks.

Then one after another in the span of three days, three members of the gang involved in the rape, including the boss of the A-Team, were found murdered near Site C. From then on the members of the gang no longer dared to move alone by day or at night. Nevertheless, a few nights later one member of the gang, stepping into the backyard of Lisa's shebeen to have a piss, did not return to his drinking fellows, and was found stabbed among the rubble later on. The last man involved in the rape then fled to Soweto, believing himself to be safe there, but he was mysteriously shot within a day of his arrival.

One cold June night the cell had staked out the house of a black councillor who had recently shot two youngsters after they threw rocks at his car on the highway which leads past the squatter camps across the Cape Flats. Although the house was well protected by a high wall, broken glass cemented into the top of the wall and barbed wire strung above it, the cell moved nearly effortlessly across this barrier, silenced the dog which had started barking loudly, and entered the dark house through one of the back windows which they cut out. There was hardly any noise as they cut and lifted the pane and squeezed through the window frame.

Lighting their torches they moved swiftly through the house which seemed deserted until they entered the bedroom, where they found the trembling wife of the councillor. They roughly ordered her to get out of the bed.

Have you no shame, she cried in tears, can't you see that I am naked.

No matter, said Ntulu, get out.

Clutching a bedsheet to her body she got up and squeezed into a corner of the room, shivering with fright in the cold winter night.

I know that you have come to kill my husband, she said. But he isn't here.

One of the group tore back the bedspread from the bed, as if he could not believe that their prey had escaped them, and looked underneath the bed.

I have told him once, and I have told him often, to keep his nose out of politics, the woman whined, and now he shoots these kids!

Shut up! growled Ntulu.

Xola looked at this woman. My mother died by some such policemen as this councillor, all traitors, helping the enemy, he
thought. They shot her, just for sports. I didn't even see her, when
they buried her. These bastards killed my mother, why should
this woman not be killed. She is on their side. She is guilty.

As if sensing what Xola was thinking, the woman suddenly
went ash-grey and shouted: I beg you, do not kill me. I beg you,
I have children like you, your age. They are at school. Please
think of your mothers.

There was a furious movement by Xola, a glint of a knife, with
lightning speed. A moment later she was bleeding from a wound
in her stomach and dying. As she lay there, her bedsheet fallen,
her brown body convulsively moving, blood spurting and then
trickling from the gash the knife had made, Xola fell into a kind
of trance.

Ntulu shook him, and said: Hey, why did you do this, you
know she didn't do anything. Xola did not answer as they led him
quickly through the back door and helped him over the wall.
Much later, as they went to sleep in their safe house, he mumbled: That was for my mother.

After this evening Xola was no longer himself. He brooded
endlessly. He started to vomit after each meal. He grew even
more silent than he had been before, seldom answering any
questions. It became obvious to his comrades that he could no
longer be trusted to lead them in their exploits, and they made
plans to hide him in a township near Worcester, in the mountains. It was not easy to make the arrangements. The father of
Ngcobo who drove a van early each morning for a Cape Town
firm, delivering fresh bread to the cafés and shops in Worcester,
was persuaded to make a detour through Guguletu and pick up
Xola. Ntulu's uncle who worked as a garden "boy" in Worcester,
had arranged for Xola to stay in the house of his sister-in-law,
Lobela.

The transport of Xola to Worcester was uneventful. He was hidden behind some crates of bread, but the van was never stopped. Lobela showed the taciturn Xola a small shack in the backyard, where he would stay, and Xola lay down on the bed, and remained motionless for hours. Sometimes he would sit in the winter sun in front of his shack and stare at the rusted iron sheets which formed the enclosure of the little yard.

There he sat, as if listening to a voice only he could hear, his eyes focused on a spot to his right, seeing an apparition only he could see, silently for many hours, not even acknowledging the presence of Lobela. Sometimes he would moan and his face would distort as if in pain.

Sometimes Lobela would hear him mumble: I was not born. I have no mother.

When he spoke, his sentences were often confused, he would break off a sentence somewhere, letting a few senseless words dangle in the air, turn around and disappear into his shack.

I need to wash off the . . . I have no . . .

Or he would make a movement as if to get up, and suddenly remain half-suspended above the rickety wooden kitchen chair for moments, as if frozen in this position. Or he would want to point to something, and his hand would remain arrested in mid-motion. Sometimes his thoughts were confused, and he did not seem to be aware that he was not at home with his parents and sisters, but with Lobela in Worcester.

Lobela noticed that Xola often had dry lips and constantly wet hands.

Most nights he would wake up, sweating and in panic, and could not go to sleep again. But he told Lobela nothing about his mental tortures.

One Sunday his two sisters came to visit him. They had hitched a ride with a priest who had come to give a sermon in the black township of Worcester. As he sat with his sisters in his shack, the August rains came pelting down and the Northeaster was howling over the flats between the mountains on which Worcester is built.

Suddenly out of the silence, he said: That woman comes every evening to demand my blood.

His sisters looked at each other: What woman?

It is the same woman but multiplied, in great numbers, and each has a bloody hole in her stomach. They are all so grey and thin, they are all so hungry, they all want to drink my blood.

What are you talking about? his sisters asked. They started to fear him, and his strange words.

I see how the floor becomes red with my blood and the women drink and drink and become more lifelike, the colour returns to their faces, and then they walk away and they seem alive.

His sisters were trying to pacify him, but he got very agitated, he started to sweat and to scream: Go away! Go away!

In the afternoon, while they were sitting and drinking hot tea made by Lobela, he suddenly said: My blood is flowing out of me. Soon my heart will stop. These old witches are sucking me dry. Then he stopped talking at all for the rest of the day. Only occasionally he put his hand to his ears, as if to stop an unbearable noise.

Before his sisters left, he rummaged among his things in his bag, took out a pencil and paper, and started to write: I have no voice any more, my life is leaving me.

Although they were quite worried about him, they had to leave, as the car of the priest was waiting in front of the house. Reluctantly they climbed into the car.

That night Xola pushed a big kitchen knife deep into his stomach. Nobody heard any noise, because of the storm. When Lobela came in the morning, his door was locked. At first she did not worry, as Xola often slept late after his sleepless nights, but when he did not appear by lunch, she broke open the door and found him lying beside the bed, naked, a jagged gash across his stomach, the knife next to his body, blood all over the floor.

Finding the truth

I AM NOT INTERESTED IN their faces. A face never tells you anything. It might look like that of the little clerk who dutifully performs his insignificant function in some dark office and who, if he votes at all, votes for the Government as dutifully as he scribbles his comments on the stacks of paper which pass through his office – and yet: he could be infected with the terrifying and all-pervading poison of the enemy. He may be plotting to overthrow the Government, to plant bombs near parliament, to organise workers to strike for a living wage, or whatever other reason they come up with to disorganise our already severely afflicted economy; he may be teaching small innocent children his poisonous doctrines, or he may be murdering faithful servants of the Government. They desecrate everything that we hold to be holy and true, they falsify our faith, they impose the tyranny of materialism, and attempt to destroy our faith in an ideal, an absolute. And yet they walk about with the most innocent faces, mimicking real human beings. No, faces lie. So I never trust faces.

If you want the truth, the real truth, the innermost truth of a person, even the methods used by the Special Branch of our police, the Special Counter-Insurgency Units, their interrogations and physical methods do not always work. Neither physical torture nor truth serums nor lie detectors are infallible. Lamentably people have held on to their inner truth even through the most scientifically organised sessions of questioning. You never know for certain what their bleeding and groaning faces are hiding, when you believe that you have extracted the last ounce of their truth from their unwilling brains and bodies. I never trust faces. Too many people I've known have hidden behind their faces. Even those who have been elected to high office sometimes hide the poison of the enemy in their brains. Faces lie. All faces lie.

The red beast with the black face is licking at all our frontiers, its seed has invaded the most innocent minds of our children, the tragedy of a noble nation to be torn down by street dogs with no conception of the nation's greatness is about to unfold before our eyes, God Himself is turning His face from a people involved in such sinful disorder, yet nobody seems to care, nobody has assigned priority funds to research the human brain, to uncover the hiding place of foreign and corrupting ideas. For years now, I have been working on a method which would be infallible. Which would tear from their brains the innermost hidden truth, the real poison that pervades the bodies and brains of most people, the pernicious doctrine which destroys anything that is decent, normal and healthy in this world. Last night, after a 24-hour session, I finally solved the riddle of the truth of a person.

Brains, like faces, look innocent. A brain is like a great soft walnut, which one can bend open in one's hands. But looking at its shimmering layers of skin, the veins and arteries which pulsed blood through the living cells, and the grey and white matter in its innocent childlike softness tells you nothing. You need the torture instruments of modern science to make them tell you their stories. And even then: most people will see nothing but cells, nuclei, ganglia. They cannot see the truth. Since yesterday I can.

I have handled more than two thousand brains the last three

years, the brains of murderers and terrorists hanged in prison, of detainees, who have died accidentally while under interrogation or have committed suicide, the brains of people who died violently and whose bodies were sent to me to determine the cause of death. But the brains do not tell the truth either. You look at them and they stare back, in all their slimy innocence. Everything in nature lies. Once you have grasped that horrible truth, you are near madness. There is nothing on which you can rely. Faces lie, brains lie, bodies lie, words lie, everything lies.

But I was sure that there would be one final place where the truth was hidden, I knew that the human soul was contained in the nerves of the body, and that in a way every nerve contains the entire spiritual being of a person, and for years I have searched for it, and now I have found it. The truth is locked away in this large steel cupboard, and I am sure if people knew that I know the truth, and that the truth is hidden in my office, they would come and murder me and destroy the last shred of evidence. Because there is one thing they cannot stand, and that is the truth. Even the police, and I do not talk about those monkeys who drive around in their jeeps and believe they are important but do not have the faintest idea of what this struggle is all about, who just like a good bash, and sometimes in their eagerness destroy the very evidence which I need to find out the truth – no, I talk about the top professionals who know all about the total onslaught, about the enemy's danger, and about the difficulty of finding out the truth, even these top people are afraid of the truth, which they are supposed to search for.

They are afraid that I might find the truth where they do not want the truth to be found. What about their own truth? They all have security clearances, but have they applied their own interrogation methods to themselves? No, everybody assumes that if you say you are a Government supporter, you really are one, if you are elected to parliament on a Government ticket, you must be a Government man, if you are made Prime Minister or State

President, you have none of the poison of the enemy in you. But of course you could be a "sleeper", a spy planted years ago by the enemy. After all, a high-ranking officer in our navy was found to be an enemy spy. So why not the Minister of Defence, or the Minister of Law and Order? That is why I have conducted my research in the last few years in total secrecy, and not even my immediate superior has the least inkling of what I am about to do. He does complain from time to time that I take too long over some of the cases, but I don't think he suspects what I am really up to. He suspects me of being lazy, of sleeping in my office, of spending afternoons in a pub, but not of having found out the truth about truth.

And yet, to know is the most important thing for man. Are we not engaged in a global struggle of good against evil, of white against black, of Christianity against the devil's forces? Is there anything more important than to win this war? If the only way to win this war is to break open skulls and tear out the brains of suspects, then we must do it. If the truth is hiding there, we must follow it into its hiding place and uncover it.

After prolonged searches in many regions of the brain, after tens of thousands of slides, stained by all the established staining methods, I began to observe a regularity in one region of the brain. Surprisingly it was very near the pituitary, in which Descartes believed he had found the interface between the soul and the mechanics of life. Just in front of and above the pituitary, towards the olfactory bulb and near the optic chiasm, I discovered the hiding place of the ultimate truth about man. I then developed a new derivative of the Golgi-stain, which selectively makes visible the truth cells. In the apparent chaos of a maze of neurons and their axons and dendrites, my new staining method brings out the clear writing of the devil. Undoubtedly I was very lucky to find those few cells amongst the hundred billion neuron cells of the brain, but I found them. I found the truth.

There remained the necessity of independent proof and of a

control experiment. I needed to kill a few people who I believed had nothing to hide whatsoever in their truth cells. Their bodies would then come back to me for dissection. My first victim was a six-year-old boy, whom I found wandering about in the bushes near the beach one Sunday afternoon. He was dead before he understood what had happened to him. I just twisted his neck. Fortunately killing children is no problem for me. I hate them and their inconsiderate noise, their harmlessness, their inability to understand the seriousness of our situation. They are, after all, not much more than wild animals who must first be drilled in the basics of our civilisation. At home in my little room near the Courts of Justice, I was overtaken by a phenomenon which I have noticed for some time. Whenever I get unduly excited, I hear a loud screaming noise for about an hour. It then dies down and I go to sleep peacefully, whereas normally I'm afraid to stop thinking in the evening. Unfortunately, this killing and a number of others in similar circumstances have created quite a furore in town, and children are more carefully watched than before, so that it becomes more and more difficult to supply innocent material for my dissections. So far, although the number of control cases is relatively limited, my theory has been borne out. The innocent do not, not yet, carry the insignia of the devil in their brains.

Two weeks ago, I was lucky enough to escape, when I sentenced and executed four young black people, who were wearing the signs of revolution openly not only in their faces, but even on their clothes. This is how far the laissez-faire attitude of the Government has brought us. Our enemies have so little fear of us that they parade the insignia of the devil, the slogans of blackness openly in broad daylight, for all to see. From my car, a nondescript grey Mazda, I fired round after round of bullets into their jerking bodies. I managed to drive off without being pursued, and I know that the police are not going to expend an inordinate amount of effort in tracing the executioner of a few revolutionary black youths. Secretly many are on my side. The bodies duly arrived in my fridges and on the slabs on which I perform my duty. I drew up my report, as required, the cause of death was obvious. What I did not mention in my report was that they were one further link in the chain of a scientific proof, and that I had killed them to provide this proof: each of them, sporting their convictions openly, showed on close dissection of the brain, the mark of the hidden truth.

Today I am going to complete the final test of my theory. I am about to leave my office. My gun is oiled and serviced. As a state pathologist I am a trusted member of the police. Nobody will suspect me. Nobody knows the truth about me. But I must know the truth about the man who governs this country. I must hold his brain in my hands, I must break it open like a walnut along its main fissure, I must dissect it under the microscope, I must find that most hidden place in the brain, where the truth resides. I am afraid. I am afraid that not even that exalted brain is free of the poison which I have discovered in all the brains I have examined so far. I am afraid that even his face lies. But I must know the truth, or I will go mad.

We must be mad

SOMEONE SHOULD HAVE TOLD THEM TO have pity on us. But they are inhuman. They don't have anything like pity in them. If they had any pity in them, then they would have answered our questions and would not have forced us to interrogate them for hours and hours on end. But as it was, they forced us to drag the information out of them piece by piece.

But you try and explain anything to them. They refuse to admit anything. They refuse point-blank. You ask them anything, and they say: I don't know. Where do you live? I don't know. Who is your commanding officer? I don't know. Who else is in your cell? I don't know. What is your name? I don't know. So, what did they expect us to do? Did they not see that they were trying to make us look ridiculous? Stupid, hard-headed nuts. I loathe them like a piece of filth, like slime, like waste or shit. They do not think of us, who must question them. Stupid uncaring lot. The lot of them.

No, I am not mad. There is really nothing the matter with me. I am twenty-eight, happily married. My wife is very understanding, although she cannot, of course, know what I had to go through. You have to go through it yourself in order to understand. The only way. But she understands, as far as anybody who has not been through this herself can. Pity, we don't have any children. Yes, we wanted to have children, but somehow we never made it. I am sorry about that. I would like to have a son. I hope we can still have children.

But my family is not my problem. The only problem with me is, I cannot sleep. I wake up with spasms in the stomach, the belly, all my intestines shrivel up, I am hollow inside, just air, like a balloon, full of air, tears streaming down my face, the taste of bile in my throat and on my tongue. Because I hear them scream. I hear how they scream, all night. My heart races like a wild machine, my hands perspire, my forehead breaks out in a sweat, the outlines of objects in the darkened room perform a dizzying dance. Vomiting, retching, my body thrusts me away from the sewage, the muck, the defilement, the shame.

Apart from that there is nothing really the matter with me. I get on with everybody, I am well-liked in the police force. My boss has always supported me. I even get on well with my in-laws, although, of course, they have no idea about the real dangers facing this country. They are the sort of nice, liberal people who believe that we can still negotiate our way out of this mess. They are against "violence". I wish they would tell the terrorists that. Really simple-minded and idealistic. But then they don't know what I know. It is no use arguing with them. And I have long given up trying to persuade them. They will see soon enough.

No, the only problem with me is, I cannot sleep at night. Even now, in summer, I close the windows, every night I put putty around all the joints of windows and doors, my wife does not understand, she complains of the heat, and, I admit it is hot, but anything is better than hearing the screams, I put earplugs in my ears, but nothing helps, the screams are there, every night. I need to throw them out of my house, but they refuse to go away. I need to make my own house at least impregnable against their nightly incursions, if we cannot seal the country against their deadly intrusions. But they do not stay out of my property, out at the edge of my garden. They enter my very bedroom with their screams. At night. An apparition, a blankness, a whiteness, faceless. Every night.

We always questioned them at night.

Sometimes I get up, turn on the radio or play records, so as not to hear this screaming all night. The neighbours have complained about the noise. But what can I do? I hear how they scream, all night. I need to drown that screaming. I am tortured by that screaming. That screaming is a hatred without words. Loathing. A loathing for us, as we loathe them.

My wife at first did not really understand. She doesn't know about the interrogations, she only complained when I had to be out at night. At one stage she believed I was having an affair. She was nagging and nagging me, it did not help when the lieutenant told her that, yes, indeed, I was working at night there. She thought he was in cahoots with me. I don't blame her. Night after night I was away, and there she was all alone. Not even a kid to keep her company. But she didn't understand. She never really understood. She doesn't understand that I cannot bear the noise of their screams.

One night she complained about the heat in the house, and about the radio, she wanted to sleep.

She said: I believe you are going mad.

I said: Fuck you, I am not going mad. It is just the screams, I cannot bear these screams. Do you hear?

Then I must have lost control of myself. Apparently I hit her, she had two broken ribs afterwards. I know nothing about it. They said I had broken her ribs. I had tied her to a chair and threatened her.

They said I screamed: I will show you who is the master here. I will show you, once and for all. Do you hear me?

Somehow I must have come to my senses before I killed her.

I found myself in the shower, when I heard her scream: Help! Help! Please, help me!

I freed her, and asked her what had happened to her. She told me.

She was frightened and said: Why don't you go and see a doctor. Your nerves, you need to do something for your nerves.

My troubles really started when I applied to be transferred to the special unit. It was stupid of me. But it seemed more interesting than tracing petty thieves and small drug peddlers. Quite exciting, like a spy novel. When they transferred me to this special unit, they at first used me to stake out suspicious places, suspected safe houses of the terrorists. Not that we discovered much. These guys are clever, and their safety is good. So we had endless boring hours sitting in cars or in rooms with a view, which we rented to spy on their comings and goings. Most of the houses we staked out were in fact really quite harmless. White student leaders playing at revolution. Not one of the big fish we knew were around organising the resistance ever showed up there. They were far too clever to walk into a trap like that. They knew that we knew. Their hide-outs were somewhere in the backyards of the townships and in the shanty towns, where we couldn't go without attracting attention. Of course, we had our black spies there, and from time to time they caught one of them. But we never got to see these killers in the places we had to watch, these killers who claim to be the saviours of the country and who are worshipped like heroes, these criminals with a good conscience, immoral, scheming, shady, these traitors, liars, these shameless rapists and murderers, terrorists that dissemble a hatred that smiles.

Then I became an assistant interrogator. I think I was a good interrogator. I got to know them better. Of course, we could not be nice to them. If you really want to find out you must not be squeamish. Occasionally, you just lose your temper, and there are broken bones, bruises, sometimes they were so badly damaged that we had to make it appear as if they had hanged themselves in their cells. Or slipped on a bar of soap in the bath. That was a funny one. It does happen, in real life. I thought of that, because when I was on the beat, we had the case of an old gentleman who actually died because he slipped on a bar of soap in his bath. Nobody believed it, of course. They never believed us. Even if for once we told the truth. But that did not matter. We knew that if we killed, we killed in the name of life, in the name of the country which gives life, in the name of an idea under attack.

In this game you cannot be squeamish. We all survived because of our unshakeable adherence to the law and to morality. I got used to the wounds with blood and pus, I got used to the stench of kaffirs, the sickly, acrid smell of sweat and fear. This is not a kindergarten, after all. This is for real. They are trying to ruin our land, and we have to do all we can to stop them. They have no feeling for what is sacred to us, our holy fatherland. They are the polluted and defiled children of Satan. They are perverts who confuse the pure and the impure, morality and immorality. There is in them one of those violent, dark revolts, directed against the forces of law and order and reason, but they are not even revolutionaries, they are an obscene joke without any rules; this whole thing, this terrorism is a convulsion that wrenches bodies in the night, a perversion, a something that I do not recognise, a meaninglessness, which crushes me, a cesspool of refuse and death. I'll do anything, anything to prevent them from reaching their objective. To exclude them, to keep them out, to draw a line. To put them behind bars like the wild animals they are. Because they want to destroy this country, my fatherland. You have to tell yourself that, you have to be quite ruthless. So if you break a few ribs that is all in the day's work. Or rather the night's work.

Because we always questioned them at night.

But they remained silent, and when we questioned them, they screamed. You had to make them scream to break their silence. They are so certain that they can endure the torture. But most of them can't. Their self-confident arrogance is soon broken down.

55

Heroes wallowing in the dirt. Suddenly ashamed of themselves, because their image of themselves is cracking.

In the beginning I liked that. The power to make them scream. It was a great feeling. I knew exactly what hurt most. What made them scream. Our relationship was unapproachable and intimate. We knew each other better than any other human being in the world. There is no knowledge like the knowledge of the torturer. And there is no knowledge like the knowledge of the tortured. Today I can tell you, as I walk past the interrogation rooms, merely by listening to their screams, at what stage of the interrogation they are.

A guy who has had his first punches from the fists of the guards screams in one way. A guy who has had a thorough beating with the sjambok has a distinctive way of screaming, talking, telling you that he is innocent, that he has nothing to do with the terrorists. If you have been suspended for two hours from your wrists, you no longer talk, but you scream like a demented night owl. After being in a wet sack and nearly choking the scream takes on a new urgency. The worst screams come after the electricity treatment. It really becomes unbearable. You think the guy is about to die, but he is not, and that is why he screams.

It is all those different kinds of screams I hear every night. That is why I cannot sleep any more. As I said, they are inhuman. They do not have any kind of pity or understanding in them. If they had any pity in them, then they would have answered our questions and would not have forced us to interrogate them for hours and hours on end.

Not all of them screamed, though. There were those who never spoke. They had heard the stories about the people who fell from the eleventh floor or were accidentally electrocuted. They came into the interrogation cell and believed that they were going to die. So in the knowledge that they were going to be killed anyway they never said anything at all. They did not even scream. They believed that we would kill them right away.

But we do not want to kill them. What we need is information. We need to understand their dark plots so as to counter them. So you have to make them scream. They must understand that they are nothing. That they are not humans. Sooner or later they start to talk after that. But why can't they just talk? It would make it so much easier for us and for them. But they remain silent until we have made them scream. Then the stories burst forth out of their unwilling mouths, always the same old stories, repetitions, nothing else. Nothing but excuses and hot air: How they suffered under apartheid. How one day they decided that they had had enough. How they organised resistance in their township. How they were recruited by the ANC or the PAC or the Communist Party. Always the same story. Unending. The dogs have compassed me, the assembly of the wicked have enclosed me.

I am not afraid of them. There is not much that they can do. But I have a fear of what they stand for. It is like a mirage, a dream image which you can never touch. They constantly ventured into that which is not tolerable or even thinkable. They were worried and fascinated by a desire which I could never fathom. When it surfaced, it sickened me, it engendered a fascination that led me towards them and revolted me at the same time. I had to reject it. Totally. Otherwise that vortex of summons and repulsion would have swallowed me entirely. This job made me sick. Perhaps I should resign from the force and work on a farm. Or learn a trade. But I am probably too old for that.

Yesterday, as I was walking through the wards, I suddenly saw him. He was lying in this white hospital bed. Motionless. His eyes staring. I recognised him immediately. My wife always says that these black faces confuse her. They all look alike. She can never remember their faces. But that is nonsense. They are as different as ours. And this face I knew. I recognised it instantly. I remembered his screams. I remembered his screams as he hit the wall. Like an animal. Like an animal about to be slaughtered.

I had never heard the screams before during the daytime. The daytime was the time for sanity and reason. No screams. But now I heard his screams as I saw him there, lying motionless. I remembered that we had to send him to hospital because after he hit the wall he was in a coma. Concussion. You become a sort of doctor. You learn about all the signs. So we had to send him to hospital.

I was shaking. I broke out in a sweat. I had not expected the screams to invade the daytime as well. I was shattered. I was really frightened.

Then the guy looked at me and recognised me. He jumped up and started to run. The warders came and began to search for him. For a long time they could not find him. Finally they found him in the toilet, where he had attempted to hang himself with his pyjama trousers. He did not succeed. Apparently he believed I had come to take him back to the interrogation cells.

The doctor told me that they had quite a job convincing him that he must have made a mistake, that no policeman was allowed to enter the hospital, that he must be exhausted, and that he was here to be treated. That he would not be sent back to prison. He never believed them. He screamed for hours: Where am I? Where am I?

Two weeks later he succeeded in hanging himself in the toilet with a piece of cord he had stolen from the morning gown of another patient.

Why can't they leave me alone? Why do they haunt me with their animal screams? Why do they not stay outside? Why do they not allow me to sleep, day and night? I sometimes ask myself why the hospital authorities allow them to come near us. There should be a line between them and us. People who have met in the way we have met in the police cells should not be allowed to meet again, outside. It is immoral. Wherever I go, however, I meet them, their faces and their screams. There is no place where they are not. It is as if they have taken over this whole universe with their screams. The whole universe thunders with their screams. The clean and proper hospital with its white sheets and immaculate nurses has become filthy, the forgotten time has cropped up and inundated these halls with muck, shit, pus, blood, vomit.

The problem is that I can't go back to the special unit to control this menace. Not as long as this sleeplessness haunts me. But I do not understand why my colleagues cannot control things any more. Are we already this weak? Helpless? Unable to stem the flood of these screaming men and women with their guns and their grinning faces, with their muck, shit, pus, blood, vomit?

Me, I am not mad, am I? I am in a deep well, in a daze, because of the many sleepless nights. I wanted to be cured of that sleepless screaming, and they sent me here, where all my words are tinged with a nothingness, a hallucination, a glimmer of light, but the light is red like blood, here, where I met this fellow, whom I had heard screaming. That did not help much, did it? Now I am like a stone before the untouchable, the impossible, the absent. Now I remain, uneasy, blank, staring at this dump of lifeless bodies, from whom I try to extricate myself. I have no other desire. I just want to be rid of these screams. I want to dig my body into the ashes of oblivion. I want to be rid of the vomit of their screams.

Oh, that was the war, you know

I WISH I STILL HAD my gun. I would shoot this bird. Popping out of its clock every quarter of an hour, plop goes the little door, and: Cuckoo, cuckoo goes the little wooden bird. Every quarter of an hour. This crazy Swiss invention for tourists who take them home to prove that they have been in Switzerland. Why my sister had to send it, I don't know. Cuckoo, cuckoo. It drives me crazy. My sister works in Geneva, at UNESCO. Has been an exile now for more than fifteen years. She also sent these miniature cowbells in different sizes with little Swiss scenes on them. And lots of other things. Although she knew that they were opening up every letter and every parcel addressed to us, she always put in these funny propaganda booklets which the UN and UNESCO printed in their war against South Africa. She knew we didn't want them. She knew that they were confiscating every one of them. But she still included them. Except when she sent presents or something valuable like the cuckoo clock or the cowbells.

My mother, of course, treasures them. Not that she ever particularly liked my sister. Or her crazy political ideas. But now that she is in exile she treasures every little present sent from Switzerland. The things are displayed all over the house. Not to talk about the practical stuff, like the mixer over there in the cupboard. Mixer, blender, shredder, liquidiser. She deals with refugees: the same guys who took their bazookas and their AK 47s and blasted all my friends to hell and high heaven. That's what they call refugees these days, bloody communist terrorists.

Like my brother, fresh out of jail, sitting around morosely, never saying a word. Even now, while I write. He just sits there and drinks coffee. All day. Doesn't talk. I don't know what he actually did to land in jail, because that was during my first stint at the border. My mother says he was just distributing pamphlets for the ANC. But hell, they don't put you in jail just for that, do they? I am sure they had their reasons, and my brother just never told my mother what really happened, so that she would not get upset.

Of course, he doesn't like me, because I have been in the army, because I am a traitor to the cause. When he was into Black Consciousness, I told him: Look here, I am no bloody black, and neither are you. We are civilised. Have been for a long time. We are not bloody kaffirs. He just looked at me, and spat on the floor. Fucking coloured! he hissed. And walked out. That is how he is.

He is still like that. Doesn't talk it out. Sits around brooding all day. Probably planning his next terrorist attack. Or how to abscond to the enemy in Botswana or Swaziland. Doesn't even go to his bloody meetings any more. Sure, he is under house arrest for three years. That does make things difficult for him, with a member of the armed forces in the same house. Ex-member. Dismembered ex-member.

But he has no feelings, no emotions. Sees me sitting here in my wheelchair, and I am sure he doesn't care a bloody hoot for his brother. Because for him I am the enemy. But then I have always been the enemy, I was the enemy long before I joined the army. I could have joined the police force then, and I would probably not have lost both legs and half an arm. But I figured at that time that I wouldn't like to shoot at people I know. At least at the border you knew who the enemy was. Although I found out they were mostly the same kind of people I would have had to shoot in Guguletu or Mitchells Plain. So, not much difference, except there they were shooting back. No "peaceful" demonstrations at the border, where all the firepower was with the police. And they didn't throw stones either. They used landmines and bazookas and Stalin organs and AK 47s, and in general were quite a dangerous lot to deal with.

Cuckoo, cuckoo goes the little wooden bird. Every quarter of an hour. You wouldn't think that a house like this with all the colour photographs on the walls, and the picture of Table Bay with white horses on the waves and sailing ships coming in, bringing a guy called Van Riebeeck who started all this mess, and with a cuckoo clock and the radio tuned to Radio Five all day long, and doilies all over the place, would produce a communist terrorist and a political exile.

Neither my father, before he died in 1977, nor my mother was ever very "political". They never went to meetings, and they did not like the "political" preachers in the African Methodist Episcopal Church, so they went to the Dutch Reformed Church, until there too the black ministers started to make political statements instead of preaching a good comforting sermon. They knew it doesn't do you any good to get involved in politics. Makes your life difficult. Especially when you are employed by the "Government". Not that my father was ever anything much in the "Government". He was a carpenter with the railways. But still, when you get your money from the "Government" you don't dabble in politics. It is unhealthy. Or get involved with trade unions. That was just looking for trouble. And he couldn't afford to get fired, not with a wife and three children to look after.

When I was sixteen, I wanted to join the railways too. But there was no job for me. So I did my matric. And then my father said: Why don't you join the Corps? Good steady job for the rest of your life. You don't have to worry.

That was fine with me. And after three years in the bush they selected me for an officer's course. They said I had leadership qualities, and the new army no longer looked at colour. The hell they did. All the plum jobs went to fucking whites. But nevertheless, I made captain. Which was not bad for a bloody coloured. And the salary, of course, was much better.

When they nabbed my brother, it didn't make my position easier. They all became very suspicious. A captain with a brother who was a convicted terrorist. Not easy, I tell you. I had to be on my guard all the time. One mistake, and they would all come down on me. And then I made the mistake, but after that it didn't much matter either way.

It doesn't pay being careless in the bush war. You walk through this dry bush, the grass up to your hips, the thorn bushes this grey-green they have in the dry season. We were not expecting any terrs in the dry season. They usually come with the rains and go with the rains. Much better cover and no problem with water. But this lot, we found out later when the army caught them, had good contacts with the locals. They moved like fish in the water, and we didn't even know they were there.

We knew that the locals were not on our side, except perhaps a few chiefs and government employees, and a few policemen. So we had real problems about who was a terrorist and who was not. The colonel reckoned that we might as well proceed on the assumption that they were all on the side of SWAPO, and treat them like that. Of course, the enemy was good on propaganda. Guys like my brother were constantly printing and distributing pamphlets. Occasionally we caught one of them, and the poor bastard usually ended up rotting amongst the bushes. Not a nice sight. But up there in the "operational area" we could not afford to play games. So, think of it, my brother got off light with seven years in prison.

Plop goes the little door, and: Cuckoo, cuckoo goes the little wooden bird, hacking my thoughts into quarter-hour-long fragments. Why do I have to have a sister in Geneva? I hate things that beep at me. Like the radio we had to carry on patrol. Base to group zero eight five. Over and out. Keep radio silence! Don't beep! Bloody cuckoo!

I was carrying the radio, although as a captain that was not my job. But I always felt that everyone should take his share of the task. On the other hand I was supposed to be up front, leading the boys. But because of the load I had trailed behind the first few guys. So when we came out of the dense bush there was this loud noise, and then for a few seconds total confusion. Hell, I am going to get those swines one day, I will never forgive them for this. There I was, and I saw Bernie explode in front of me. Yes, like his arms came hurling towards me. I was in fact holding his arms in my arms. There his body was exploding, ribs, heart, lungs flying about. I could see in slow motion as his body expanded, expanded, expanded and then burst. And all the time I was running towards Bernie, running, running, but it made no sense. Hell, I will never forget how Bernie exploded, I mean he was hit by a panzer grenade. And as I ran towards him, there was this machine-gun fire, the pieces of shell whizzing through the air. I screamed, but by that time I could not hear myself, later I knew my ears were full of blood, as I fell, with Bernie's arms in my arms, I fell and lost consciousness for a moment.

I still wake up, bathed in sweat, when my dream breaks off at this moment. Every night. Sometimes twice or three times. I don't think I will ever forget this image of Bernie exploding, not if I live to a hundred. Not ever. Nor will I forget the hours when I was lying in the sun, thinking I was going to die.

And to think that guys like my brother, who sits here drinking his coffee, were responsible for it! It is hard not to be able to get up and strangle him. Slowly. The swine! It is bitter not to be able to jump up and have a go at him. Oh, he knows that I hate him. For what they did to me, and the others. Ronnie, Lefty, Charles, Rashid, Muggsy. He knows I can never forgive him. Him, and his crazy dream of overthrowing this Government.

When I came to, bloodbubbles were forming in front of my mouth, filling themselves with speech, unintelligible, bursting in frayed droplets. So much to say, but no way of saying it. Nobody to listen to me anyway. Yet in all this emptiness the urge to speak thoughts, which ended up in pink-coloured balloons, which were constantly bursting in front of my mouth. Gagged. The nauseous taste of sweat and bile. Talk. Want to talk. Want to say how it is. The tongue moving against the wet cloth. Bile rising. Choking. I want to speak. I want to speak against this gag in my mouth. I want you to hear the voices. I want you to hear and to see. I want to eject this gag, choking me, from my mouth. I want to free my tongue, so that you can hear. I want to free my hands. I want to use these hands. I want to tell it as I see it. Talk. I want to talk about it. I must talk about it. I want to travel through this silence and fill it with my voice. I want to run away from this light which stabs into my eyes. Everywhere I turn in this narrowness there is me and me and me. I want to get out of me. I want to make my voice speak of all that has happened. I want the other voices to speak and I want to take up their melody and follow the line of their vowels to their thoughts. But I gag. I vomit into the stiff cloth filling my mouth. And in the silence there is nobody but my shadow wreathing on the floor. The sharp shadow in contortions, vomiting endlessly and silently. Eating its own vomit. Vomit in my lungs. Blinding stabs through my chest. I. We. Want. To talk. No longer. To take a knife and cut through the gag. Cut open the sealed mouth. Bleeding, it talks. Another mouth. My mouth. Dirt encrusted.

Those were the worst five hours of my life, as I lay all alone in the red dust, and was slowly bleeding to death, or so I thought. I did lose a lot of blood. I was totally dehydrated from the heat, and unable to reach my flask. I heard the radio talk, but could not answer. I have never been able to speak about these hours. To anybody. That experience is burned into my memory, and it replays itself like a tape, again and again. It comes to haunt me day and night. A sudden spell of dizziness, a certain pallor, the fear that grips my stomach, the fright. The need to scream in all this horror, but the scream remains silent. I have never been able to remove that gag out of my mouth. The dryness of the throat has remained with me.

They got me out of there, later, they must have heard the signal from the radio, for I had thrown the panic switch as I fell, and they came with three helicopters, but all my men were killed or wounded, and we had to let the swine get away with it. They flew me to Windhoek, and then to Cape Town. The butchers in Windhoek cut off the frayed pieces which had once been my legs, and half my arm. In Cape Town they treated me for shell-shock, and taught me how to use a wheelchair.

They gave me a good pension, all right. I mean, I can live. I don't live in luxury, seeing that my brother does not go to work, can't go to work because he is under house arrest, and that my mother gets a small pension from the railways, not enough for her to live on. But we can all live on my pension. It is an irony that the state in effect pays a pension to a convicted terrorist, at least indirectly, but such is life in this crazy country.

Here it goes again: Cuckoo, cuckoo. I could shoot this bird. Popping out of its clock every quarter of an hour: Cuckoo, cuckoo. Every quarter of an hour. Maddening. Will make me go out of my mind one day. I don't know what I'll do. This bird, and my brother.

It would all be bearable, if my brother were not here, sitting on the other side of the table, drinking coffee. Silently. Sometimes I wonder whether my brother has a gag similar to mine in his throat, throttling all attempts to speak about his horror. Perhaps that is so. I wonder what they did to him in his prison, so that he lost the power to speak. But then I think, it's his own bloody fault. Why did he have to mess with the Government. My father always told us, it doesn't pay to mess with the Government.

Every day I write this story down in my head. Every day. Over and over again. Every day I write it down on a sheet of paper in my tiny handwriting which fills the page from margin to margin in a spiderweb of words. Every evening I tear up what I have written, while my brother watches me, unmoved, stolid.

But today was different. While I was still writing, my brother threw his coffee cup at the cuckoo when it popped out for its five o'clock call: four high and five low cuckoos. The clock suddenly stopped. The bird call was silenced.

Fucking bloody cuckoo clock! he shouted.

It seems we have at least one thing in common.

With that he got up, and shouted: I wish you would stop scribbling your fascist memoirs! and walked out.

Well, at least he talked to me. And he got up from his bloody chair. Perhaps there is hope for the two of us.

The equality treatment centre

THEY CAME ONE FRIDAY AND took me away from my family to the Equality Treatment Centre, because, they said, my size and weight offended the starving masses. It is obscene, the Chief Equaliser said, to be fat like you, when the great majority of our people run around with their ribs sticking out in the glaring sunlight.

My wife and my children were crying, but the Equaliser crew just pushed them aside. I was unable to move: fear had immobilised me. I imagined they would take me as they used to take dogs on the street to the SPCA, there to be killed, if nobody claimed them within a certain space of time.

One of the crew made an obscene joke about how my virility would be restored in the Equality Treatment Centre. It works wonders, he said laughing. Just take away all this fat, and he will be like new. He will want to screw you every ten minutes.

The others roared with laughter.

Have you no shame, my wife shouted, don't you see these are innocent children? And anyway, what nonsense is this: an Equality Treatment Centre! People are different. They come in all sizes. You can't make them equal.

Woman, you are blaspheming against the fundamental wisdom

of our Elder Statesman, the Chief Equaliser said to my wife. That precisely is the problem: that people insist on being different. We need to eradicate all differences to create a just and democratic state.

But what shall we do? my wife wailed. How shall we survive? Don't you understand? We need our father! Who is going to provide for us? We will all die of hunger.

Don't be selfish, the Chief Equaliser said to my wife. We only do what is socially necessary. We need to eliminate envy in our society. And looking at your husband, it does not seem that this family is dying of hunger. You should see the children in the shacks out on the Flats!

Oh, we will all die! my wife howled, and all the children looked scared and began to cry.

Now I do admit that I have a grotesque figure, but until then it had earned me amused laughter or disgusted snorts, at best the pity of onlookers. Until then I had not met anybody who actually *envied* me. But these were the times of revolution, and all things changed, and so I supposed I would have to change with them.

Not that I hadn't tried before. Being fat like me is not really all that comfortable. But the countless diets I had tried had never helped, because it is the hormones, as my doctor used to say, good old Dr Hamcut, bless his soul. Every time I lost about four kilos, which is nothing in relation to my total weight, and before I knew, not only did I have them back on again, but an extra kilo on top of it. So eventually I gave up. Might as well stay fat without the hassle and the bother of keeping to a diet.

So here I sat in this special structurally strengthened vehicle, and was transported to the Equality Treatment Centre. The rumours I had heard about it were frightening enough: in the Size and Weight Section, where I was going, it was believed that they made you fast for however long it took for you to come down to what they had decreed was an "equal" weight. Fast! Not diet! No food at all, just water. An enforced, prolonged hunger strike! As

I thought about it, I started to cry. No more chocolates, no more steaks, no more cream cakes, not even potatoes, not even dry bread. Just nothing. The full enormity of what they intended doing to me hit me squarely. I started to howl like a wolf, wallowing in self-pity.

The Equality Treatment Centre is an enormous complex. It is an immense machine: a factory to produce equals. Its entrance gate looks like a castle or a fortress, a phony imitation of the fort in Cape Town, with observation posts all over the place. It looks like a high-security prison with five-metre-high walls, glass shards on them, razor wire all over the place, thick steel gates and clanging steel-grilled doors. I had heard about this place, but the reality was even worse than my worst dreams. One look at this building, and I knew they meant business. No pity here! I knew I was going to die of hunger. The bastards were going to let me die of hunger. And nobody would even know!

The car stopped. The gate clanged open. We drove past the gate, the gate clanged shut. The main road stretched for miles. From time to time a side road led to a huge complex of buildings. There were signs: Creativity Equalising Centre, Intelligence Equalising Centre, Aggressivity Equalising Centre, Sportsmanship Equalising Centre, Sexuality Equalising Centre, and a lot more gibberish like that. Finally we stopped in front of a huge building with the sign: Weight Equalising Centre.

The Equaliser crew helped me out of the vehicle. The Chief Equaliser spoke through an intercom to the right of the enormous steel door: New patient. A squeaky loudspeaker replied: Coming, coming. The steel door opened, creaking on its hinges. A muscular man took me by the arm and pulled me inside. The steel door was shut again.

So, here I was, in the infamous Equality Treatment Centre.

The corridors were of that nondescript vomit-coloured oil paint which is typical of hospitals and other state institutions. Vomit made me think of eating. After the long journey I was ravenous. I mentioned this to my guard, but he just glowered at me: Silence! he whispered. I started to cry again.

He led me along the corridor towards an elevator, and went up to the fifteenth floor with me. Another slow, painful waddle through a corridor. Taking out a key, he opened the door of room no. 1532.

This is going to be your home, he said, until you are equalised. With that he pushed me through the doorway. The room was bare. There was a plastic bed but no mattress, bedspread or cover on it. A table. Plastic. A chair. Plastic. A screen. Plastic.

You must undress, the guard said. We have had cases where people under treatment started to eat their shoes and their clothes.

I am not undressing in front of you, I shouted. I refuse. I will have my human dignity respected. I refuse. Do you hear, I refuse.

He shrugged, went outside into the passage and came back.

We are all equal, he said. Don't make a fuss. Underneath our clothes we are all equal. It is time you began to understand this.

I still refused to undress. I hated my naked self, and I would definitely not show it to a sneering warder. I hated all this wobbly fat. Yes, I wanted to be equal. But not this torture, this starvation, this jail, this institution. Of course, I have to admit, I couldn't do it on my own. But there must be another way.

In five minutes there were four more of his type. Three of them held me down, while the other two quickly undressed me. Then they left me there in the middle of the room: naked.

I did not know where to look: I detested all these fat rolls, the wobbly breasts, the huge rolls on my arms, my bulging stomach with its hundreds of folds obscuring the view down to my sex. Haven't seen my sex for decades! Somewhere below my stomach there must be two pillars of legs. Out of view! Oh yes, I wanted to be equal. I did not want to see this, for ever and ever.

The space of a prison cell was both hostile and familiar. I had known it from that first day when my father locked me in my room for a whole afternoon for stealing two apples from the neighbour's orchard. Being locked up became familiar in school: for not having done your homework, for talking in class, for being involved in a fight during the break. Being in a confined space, your appetites confined. Not doing or eating what you like. I walked two steps and was in the middle of the cell. It was quiet, and there was the smell of ammonia and sweat. I wanted to scream, but nobody came, and I remained alone in my cell. There was only the plastic bed, the plastic table, the plastic chair, and the plastic screen.

I sat down on the plastic chair, which creaked under my weight, and wept again. Finally I decided to lie down on the bed. I was still ravenously hungry. I dozed off. When I woke up I discovered that I was sucking my thumb. Now I was thirsty as well. I discovered a toilet with a washbasin behind the screen in the corner of my cell, and greedily drank water. It filled my stomach. But it did not make the hunger go away.

Some time later I must have fainted. When I woke up it was already dark. I got up and groped my way to the door. I stood leaning against the iron of the door, I felt the coldness spreading through my body, I felt the emptiness of my bowels, they screamed hunger, and I started to bang on the door.

Open up, I am hungry, I shouted.

Nobody answered. My words bounced off the walls and the iron door.

I shouted and banged until a guard came and gave me an injection.

Again I collapsed and lost consciousness, my ears filled with the sound of the door shutting.

I woke up during daytime. I dozed off again. My stomach felt like an enormous hole. Screaming at me to be fed, to be filled. With anything. I was prepared to eat plastic. But the bed, the chair, the table were solid, and my teeth made no impression, not even a mark.

Later that day one of the guards brought me a booklet. Made of plastic!

Equality, the cover stated. *The philosophy of our society. The thoughts of the Elder Statesman.*

I had read this thing dozens of times. Every citizen must have a copy of it. It is required reading in our schools. There are regular reading groups, where every citizen must show up at least once a year to refresh his knowledge of this, the basic law of our society. Up to now I had never really taken the book seriously. It seemed like idealistic twaddle to me: "The true and only virtue," this great philosopher wrote for example, "is, therefore, to hate ourselves (for our appetites make us hateful), and to look for a truly lovable being, in order to love him." Of course, that being was the Elder Statesman. But now, in this bare room, weeping, howling with anger, hunger, frustration, for the first time I understood that the Elder Statesman meant every word of it. Every single word. And that I was the object of that philosophy, if you can call this nonsense philosophy, and now "my hands are tied and my mouth is gagged".

Of course, we all subscribed to the principle of equality. We knew what it meant to be treated as non-equals, and we valued our equality above all things in the world. Our equality was the basis of our freedom. But I had always thought that the nonsense which our Elder Statesman had penned during the time in exile was not taken seriously by anybody.

It hardly needs to be said that there had been rumours about the Equality Treatment Centre. But again, we were assured by the mass media that only people who grossly violated the principle of equality were taken there to be "straightened out". Until I was taken there I did not see myself as violating the principle of equality. I did not feast on caviar, crayfish or twenty-five-year-old bourbon, did I? I did not eat more (well, not much more) than anybody else I knew. I was not an enemy of society. Or was I?

It seemed I was. Merely because I weighed four times as much as the average citizen, I had violated the principle of equality by having hormones which made me fat. This was ridiculous.

I hammered against the door again, screaming: Guard, guard!

I decided that my incarceration in the Equality Treatment Centre must be a mistake. I would appeal against it.

After much hammering against the door, a guard opened. In his hand was an injection needle.

Stop, I cried. I want to appeal. Get me paper and pen.

You want to appeal, he laughed. On what grounds?

On the ground that there must be a mistake. I have never violated the principle of equality in my life.

Oh, he laughed louder, look at you! Look at you! You have never violated the principle of equality in your life. Yet one merely needs to look at you. Your very body is a violation of the principle of equality. Now stop bothering me. Sit down and do some hard dieting, so that your body no longer violates the principle of equality.

With that he banged the door shut.

I looked at my offending body. It was an assault on the basic law of our society. It seemed as if I had to accept this. I was a criminal. Or rather my hormones were criminal. I hated my hormones, and I hated my body. I hated this mass of flesh which was incarcerating me.

How I survived the next forty-eight days I do not know. I spent most of my time lying on my bed, too weak to move my body which refused to melt away. I lost about ten kilos the first week, twelve the second week. I started to eat my own excrement. But there was less and less of it. I fasted, I was hungry, I fainted. But I still could not see my legs. The folds of my stomach grew more complex, but the size of it was still enormous. The skin of my arms started to wrinkle, but they still looked more like the legs of other people than like arms.

The next two weeks I was mostly unconscious. In the fifth

week I awoke once lying on a hospital bed with various wires and drips attached to me. I was too weak to ask what the drips fed into me. Probably just water. They were really hard here. No let-up until you were equal. Of the sixth week I remember nothing. I must have been in a continuous coma.

When I woke up I did not recognise myself. Although my lower body was covered with a white sheet, I could actually see my toes sticking up under the sheet. I had become equal.

They had fed me sucrose, they said, just enough to keep me alive, not to make me fat again. I was allowed to drink some soup made of vegetables. Half a cupful, which I threw up instantly, then later that evening a whole cup. The next day some maize porridge without salt or seasoning. Slowly I recovered.

But I was weighed carefully every day to see that I did not gain weight again.

As soon as I could walk, I was made to attend the equality lessons. The lessons consisted of endless repetitions of *Equality, the philosophy of our society* by the Elder Statesman, and some practical brainwashing about the diet we would have to follow from now on: one cup of bouillon in the morning, one at lunch and some maize porridge in the evening. Plus as much green salad and carrots as we wanted to eat.

In order to keep our minds away from the thought of eating we were required to take part in all kinds of activities: therapy by being occupied. Unfortunately I noticed too late that every one of these activities was in fact a disguised equality test. There were games which automatically rated your intelligence or your conformity to the norms of society, and the painting and wood-work classes somehow revealed my creativity and my sex-drive ratings. And of course the ball games, the mini golf and the therapeutic swimming showed up my total inability to move in the way required by any sport.

I was soon to find out that I was a nearly hopeless case of in-equality.

One morning after musical chairs, the Chief Equality Officer called me into his office, and told me gravely:

We had hoped that we would be able to discharge you in a week's time. But unfortunately, we have discovered other serious deviations from the norm in our tests. Your IQ is 125, and that is fifteen points above the maximum allowed. Your creativity index is 257, and that is positively abnormal, I would even say pathological, that is, what we call a habitual criminal rating.

I collapsed, and cried again.

Weeks and weeks, perhaps even months or years of Equality Treatment Centre lay ahead of me. I could not bear it. I crawled into my cell and slept.

To make it short: I spent another two years and seven months in treatment.

I was shunted from the Creativity Equalising Centre to the Intelligence Equalising Centre and back.

I soon learnt not to say anything more intelligent than the average guy with an IQ of 100. I also learnt never to come up with a solution to a problem which was more innovative than what the average party hack or doctor of the revolution would be able to think up.

One of my fellow inmates, Domino, had a much harder, not to say an impossible task: with an IQ of 85 he had to simulate one of 100. Most of the time he did not even understand what they wanted of him. It soon became clear to me that they would have to keep him in until the end of his life, poor guy. He could read and write his name after four months' training, and that was about it. But to our surprise, after another three months he was declared equal and released.

Some people despite their intelligence did not fare as well as he or I did. Berillo, for example, the poor guy was a genius. He had an IQ of 215, must have been one of the most intelligent beings on earth. But he could not control his urge to doodle. They caught him again and again trying to solve some intricate equations in higher mathematics which even Professor Matthew of the South Western University (an expert on populist arithmetic, who was called in to consult with the equaliser) could not solve, didn't even understand.

How can you be so stupid, when you are so intelligent? I mean it is not so difficult to pretend that you are stupid, if you are intelligent. But he just could not do it.

Sometimes, when we were allowed to walk in the spacious park of the Intelligence Equalising Centre, he would take me aside and confide in me: The real individual today can only live in jails like these. The place for the individualist today is in jail.

I pretended that I did not understand him.

Or do you deny that this place of mechanised madness is a jail? This place conceived in a mean calculation how best to enfeeble, stupefy and numb us, the prisoners? Admittedly, it looks like a sanatorium, and we are allowed to walk around in the park, but did you see the walls and the gates when you came in?

But this is merely an institution to make us equal, it is for our own good, isn't it? The walls are there to protect us against the envy of the equals.

He shook his head, and said: Look, you are more intelligent than that. Why do you pretend that you are as stupid as this lot, who do their best to deprive us of intellectual exercise, prohibit any study, don't allow us to read anything other than the mind-deadening novels of their prison library? Come on, use your brain, don't let them intimidate you!

I remained silent.

Think! he said, think!

I shook my head in desperation. I wanted to get out of here. And I knew that thinking would not get me anywhere. At least not the kind of thinking he had in mind. I had to be equal. To be equal was my only chance of escaping a hell, where I had to eat one cup of bouillon in the morning, one cup of bouillon at lunch and some tasteless maize porridge for dinner. I wanted to return to the world of chocolates, steaks, legs of lamb, pork cutlets, cream cakes, smoked salmon and Rhine Riesling. I did not want to become a bloody martyr of my intelligence.

To arrive at the truth, he continued, we have to give our voice to suffering. Suffering is the objective truth of this life. We need to speak of suffering. We need to speak the truth. Even if they have to liquidate us.

You've lost me, I said, this is much too academic for me.

If we silence suffering, he continued, we are accomplices of those who make us suffer. Even in jail we must pronounce our suffering. And we suffer, because we refuse to become equal. Never! Never! Never will I become equal!

This man is crazy! Doesn't he understand that the only way out of here is not to pronounce anything? Least of all the blasphemous desire to be unequal?

The moment you deny that you suffer, and the moment you deny that you are different, they have you. The moment you get out of this jail, you are dead.

I do not follow your paradoxes, I said. The moment I get out of this jail, I will be equal and alive. I live for that moment, when I will see my wife and children again.

Look, why are you so afraid? he sighed. There is nothing to be afraid of. You will be in a jail outside as much as inside. Your fear of thinking arises out of your passions. I know that really you are craving food. Your reason urges you to think in contravention of the laws of equality, and yet you find it impossible because you think of steaks and cakes. But as soon as you start eating again, as soon as you start thinking again, as soon as you start solving problems again, as soon as you start enjoying sex and sexual fantasies again, you will be back here in no time. So why not stay here and be free.

How can you be free here? I asked, but immediately understood my mistake. If anyone overheard me, that could cost me another year of indoctrination.

This jail is the only place you can be free in these days, he laughed. This jail is a hell in which to explore your intellect in joyous contravention of the laws of equality. You see, they have always stuck people like you and me into hell. But hell is merely an absurd machine for breaking the likes of us.

I walked away. The man was not only a genius and crazy. He was downright dangerous.

As I walked away, he shouted: Critical thought is an absolute necessity. You cannot run away from it without damaging yourself. Think! I tell you: Think!

But I didn't answer him. I did not pronounce. Anything.

I kept silent, except for the inanities required to make me appear equal.

I was eventually released. Berillo remained inside.

As soon as I was released, I went shopping with my wife: we bought caviar, smoked salmon, a large leg of lamb, potatoes and asparagus, ice cream and chocolate cream cake, all the things I had dreamt about for years in the Equality Treatment Centre, and that evening we had a feast of culinary delights, making up for all the bland maize porridge I had eaten, compensating me for the hunger and pain of the Equality Jail.

As Berillo had said, I started thinking again as soon as I had eaten. I eat, therefore I think, therefore I am. I started reading books which I had never before even looked at. Finally, quite by chance, I discovered a library in an old and overgrown garden, a place that had somehow been forgotten by the equality police. An old man named Theodore fearfully opened the door. For many years I had walked past this garden and not seen the little metal plaque that said it was the home of the Elitist Philosophy Museum. In the entrance hall was a display of the deformed and decidedly unequal physiognomies of the ancient philosophers, designed to instil shock and abhorrence in the minds of the equal. But so depraved was I by then that I recognised my soul brothers, and began a binge of joyful reading.

Thus, eating and reading, I slowly returned to my previous size and weight. It was inevitable, and finally it happened. They came again and took me to the Equality Treatment Centre. It is shocking, the Chief Equaliser said, to be fat like you, when you were given the chance to reduce your obscene fatness once before. They also knew about my visits to the Elitist Philosophy Museum. My wife and my children were crying, because they knew that this time I would be held for much longer. But I accepted my fate. As Berillo had said: we suffer, because we refuse to become equal. And I resolved silently and blasphemously: Never! Never! Never will I become equal! They believe and they claim that this jail produces equals. I knew now: No such thing is produced. They try to break you down here, to crush you, to make you fit into the holes they have created as a means of measuring equality. But people leave here, and they still do not fit. So they come back again and again. Because this jail is the only place where they can live. The real individual today can only live in jails like these. The place for the individualist today is in jail.

Berillo, of course, does not have the same problems that I have. He just craves to think, and that he can do in the Equality Treatment Centre as well as anywhere else; he does not crave as I do caviar, crayfish or twenty-five-year-old bourbon, smoked salmon, a large leg of lamb, potatoes and asparagus, ice cream and chocolate cream cake, steaks, pork cutlets, and Rhine Riesling. It will be hell. But it will be worth it.

Practical criticism

THE PROBLEM WITH ELISE WAS her critic. He just could not manage to write her into fame. His name was Charles, and maybe that had something to do with his inability to write in such a way as to make people want to buy her books. His hyperboles of praise were soaked with defeat. There are reviews like that. However good the book: it is doomed by the praise of reviewers like Charles.

Elise lived in an old flat near the city with a bed, a two-plate stove, a desk and a typewriter. The rooms of the flat were smaller than the rooms in other flats. That does of course narrow down the choices of a writer when she sits at her desk and tries to write a story or a poem, because you need some room in which to move your elbows when you want to write down certain words which are not usually used in flats like that. But on the other hand she had developed a mastery over the words that were possible within the confines of her flat and she had even made this mastery over the limitations of her flat a special mark of her style, which made it unlike the style of everyone else writing in Cape Town at the time.

Charles was not young any longer. He was chubby and rosy-cheeked with a few grey strands in his hair, which receded from his forehead, giving him the air of an intellectual, capable of deep thought. At the same time he gave an impression of prim rotundity.

It was well known in literary circles that Charles sometimes slept with the object of his criticism; what was less well known was that he always wore a white surgeon's mask when he entered Elise's bedroom in the nude, and intoned a long lament which always ended in the words: You are confusing me with somebody else. Despite his claims about his far-reaching pen, his performance in bed was on the whole just adequate. Which explains why these get-togethers did not take place more often. The small size of the flat may have been an additional factor. It was not conducive to wild orgies.

It is certain, however, that the erotic descriptions in her novels, poems and short stories were unrelated to reality. Not even the most credulous believed that Charles in any way resembled the macho heroes of her fictional love life. In her circles it was also generally accepted that the poet needs to endure deprivation in order to become creative, and the very lack of real stimulation in her life may have induced the rich colorations of her descriptions. But, as I said before, it was all to no avail, as very few people showed any willingness to buy her new books, which her indulgent publisher printed once a year as regular as clockwork. Maybe she should have looked for another lover and critic. But then there were very few critics around who owned a silver BMW. If, like Elise, you do not own a car and cannot drive one, that is a consideration.

Elise's mother was an obsessional neurotic who was under treatment at Valkenberg. She regularly sent Elise baby dresses to remind her of her duty as a wife and mother. But Elise was not married and had no intention of becoming a mother. Since the age of fifteen she had been well versed in all the available implements for contraception and was not averse to using them on the regular but rare occasions where they were called for. Elise's mother also loved cats and sent her postcards depicting cats in various poses about once a week, with admonitions to always water her plants and to think of England. Once a month she admonished her to remember her happy youth in the small house in Rondebosch, and to provide her husband and her children with as much happiness as she, the mother, had given to her, Elise.

Elise collected all the cat postcards in a big shoebox. The most recent one was pinned on the door to the toilet. Elise never wrote to her mother, because she saw her childhood differently. Her main problem at the moment, anyway, was her critic. She was seriously considering trading in her elderly model for a more dashing younger critic with a Volksie. She hesitated, because she was not sure whether she would be able to survive the emotional and physical stress that goes with such an affair. Young people tend to be very demanding. But she knew that her fame needed to be established now or never.

As she scanned the local newspapers for reviews she came across the initials AF under a review written with great enthusiasm. It was a novel which Charles had slated in another local newspaper a week before. As she read, she heard a voice which inspired her with confidence. It was clear to her instantly that anybody who read this review would buy the book. A week later she asked her local bookseller whether that particular book had been selling well recently. It had. There were stacks of the novel in the bookshop and the shop assistant confirmed that they were picked up at the rate of one per hour. Which was unheard-of in Cape Town.

Elise decides to track down the anonymous AF. The *Cape Times* is reluctant to lift the secrecy. Elise leaves a note addressed to AF with the editor, containing an invitation to meet her for tea on the waterfront. AF phones and says she is interested. Her name is Annemarie Farque. They meet at the waterfront and Elise is convinced. Annemarie is convinced. They move into a flat in

PETER HORN

Gardens, and start AE Creative Enterprises Inc. AE Creative
Enterprises Inc. is a success. Charles is retrenched.

Charles now writes slating reviews of Elise's work in the
Weekly Mail. He should have done this earlier, because there is a
sudden spurt of interest not only in her current novel, entitled
Chains of Blood, but in her entire oeuvre. Her first novel, *Inside
My Uterus*, first becomes a South African bestseller, then wins
the Forgotten Great Novels Prize of the Michigan Literary
Society. Charles is booed by the literary establishment as a de-
structive, arrogant and elitist critic, but is able to buy himself a
Mercedes, and acquires a new object for his criticism: Malva van
Straaten, whose first novel, *Winter of Disgust*, has sunk without
a trace. People say that the problem with Malva van Straaten is
her critic. But that is another story. Except that she never shows
the independence of mind to look for another critic, even when
Charles goes to jail later on, and so she never wins the Forgotten
Great Novels Prize of the Michigan Literary Society. Nor the
Weltfriedenspreis of the Association of German Booksellers, nor
an honorary doctorate from the State University of Oklahoma.
Bad luck.

Elise in the meantime struggled with the size of the new flat in
Gardens. The rooms of the flat were larger than the rooms in
other flats. That does of course widen the choices of a writer
when she sits at her desk and tries to write a story or a poem, because you need some room in which to move your elbows when
you want to write down certain words which are only possible in
flats like that. But on the other hand she had developed a mastery
over the words which were possible within the confines of her
previous flat and she had even made this mastery over the limitations of that tiny place a special mark of her style, which made
it unlike the style of everyone else writing in Cape Town at the
time. She now had to acquire a mastery over her new vocabulary,
and convince people that she had created a new, equally unique
style.

84

With the appearance of her next book, a collection of short stories called *Sharing My Rug*, critics noted that Elise lived in a universe of pessimism, but pessimism and cynicism were fashionable at the time among white readers, who watched with horror the impending possibility that the ANC would nationalise their swimming pools and CD players. Yet the book did not even mention the fact that her universe was populated by people other than white-skinned ones. The short stories were concerned with her obsessive attempt to insure language against the total indifference of the universe. They revolved around the debasement of language as a means of certainty about the real world. The universe seemed to her like an enormous simulacrum of a reality without reality. That uncertainty incited her to bring forth cascades of words, overflowing pages and pages of paper. The pages of her short stories covered the walls and the floors of her study. One night she tore them all down and was just about to burn them in the fireplace when Annemarie came in and saved the book from total destruction.

Sharing My Rug was an instant success. AF's review was enthusiastic. Charles gleefully pointed out that whereas Elise had been incompetent before, her new collection of short stories was totally hopeless. A week later she asked her local bookseller whether her book was selling. It was. There were stacks of the book in the bookshop and a special display in the window, and the shop assistant confirmed that it was being picked up at the rate of two per hour. Which was unheard-of in Cape Town. Of course, it helped that Charles had insinuated that she lived in a lesbian relationship with her critic, AF, and that the book gave titillating details of that affair.

It is well known in literary circles that AF sometimes sleeps with the object of her criticism; what is less well known is that they do nothing more than hold each other's hands and look into each other's eyes while exploring each other's astral souls. It is certain, therefore, that the erotic descriptions in Elise's short stories are unrelated to reality. But people who read Charles's review are convinced. The book is a bit of a disappointment, since only the title story deals explicitly with a lesbian affair.

Of course, Annemarie cannot live by writing reviews about her object of criticism alone. She has to make a living, and the flat in Gardens is more expensive than the flat she lived in before. She writes about the hole in the ozone and the plight of the penguins, and about the skin cancer of sea elephants. She breaks into the *Sunday Times* and finally gets a column on green affairs in the *Sunday Times Magazine*. She now signs with her full name and drives a BMW. Elise still cannot drive. She is convinced that learning to drive would interfere with her creative abilities. Besides, she has failed the driving test eight times already. Which convinces her of her creative abilities.

Elise's mother, who has somehow heard about her success, sends Elise baby dresses to remind her of her duty as a wife and mother. But Elise has no intention of becoming a mother. She is still exploring her astral soul with Annemarie. Elise's mother also sends her postcards depicting cats in various poses about once a week, with admonitions to remember her happy youth in the small house in Rondebosch, and to provide her mother with as much happiness as she, the mother, had given to her, Elise. She obviously needs money. Elise never writes to her mother, because she sees her childhood differently, but she sends an occasional ten-rand note. She remembers how her father used to beat her up every Saturday when he came home from the pub. Sometimes he also beat up her mother. She does not believe that she had a happy childhood. Secretly she grants her mother the right to have different memories, even if these memories do not coincide with reality as she sees it. But she decidedly does not want to enjoy a happy family life.

While Annemarie was investigating the hole in the ozone and the skin cancer of sea elephants in the Antarctic, Elise entered into an affair with Vincent, a young black student who had attended one of her readings and book-signing sessions. She had always been against apartheid, and now felt it her moral duty to give a signal to that effect as a writer and as a human being. Apartheid had been declared officially dead by that time and Nelson Mandela had been released from prison, but she believed there was still much to be done to eradicate it in practice. She was heroically prepared to contribute to that process. She also noticed that Vincent was very good-looking. The affair lasted for one week. It was very turbulent, and provided Elise with the material for her most daring novel, *You Have No Colour*. In essence, the book recounts her disappointment with the fact that Vincent in no way approached her dream of the native son: he was unable to enlighten her about the initiation rites in which she was interested as a writer and he had an undergraduate degree in literature and religious studies and was as blasé and boring as any other student of his age. He was also a very reborn Christian, and very uncertain about his sexual preferences, if any. Most of the time he read William Blake, on whose work he intended to write his MA. In the week they spent together she could get him to overcome his moral inhibitions only once. For the rest of the time he slept in Annemarie's room with the key turned in the lock.

The novel was hailed by AF as the greatest masterpiece of South African fiction, worthy of the Nobel Prize, and by Charles as the most insincere and inept piece of writing he had ever come across. The book received the Weltfriedenspreis of the Association of German Booksellers for its contribution to overcoming racial prejudice in the land of apartheid. The State University of Oklahoma awarded her an honorary doctorate in recognition both of her literary talent and her daring exploration of a theme of universal significance.

When Elise returned from the United States, Charles came to see her at the flat in Gardens. He congratulated her on her prize and on the honorary doctorate. Elise was furious. How dare you, she said. Malva van Straaten had in the meantime written her second novel, *The Black Hole*, and had set off on a holiday in Europe financed by her father, who was a rich wine farmer from the Paarl area. Charles had his monthly desire, and indicated this desire to Elise. Elise was reluctant. Charles persisted. After a bit of a struggle, the two of them landed up in bed. Annemarie, when she found them there, declared the intercourse to have been a rape. Elise testified in court that it was a rape. Annemarie testified in court that it was a rape. Charles was sentenced to six years' imprisonment.

Malva van Straaten returns from Europe and is inconsolable. Because Charles went to bed with Elise. But mainly because Charles is in prison. She is prepared to forgive him. But not Elise. She starts a campaign of revenge in the *Vrye Weekblad* and *Die Burger*. The campaign has little effect, since Elise's readers do not read the *Vrye Weekblad* and *Die Burger*. Elise completes her next novel: *Male Madness*. Of course, everybody recognises Walter, the rapist, whose sexist interior monologue forms the main body of the novel. Dirty talking, pathological self-esteem covering a total nonentity, babbles for five hundred pages through a meaningless universe filled with the most detailed description of the anatomy of human beings, both male and female. Walter is a closet fascist. Walter is in love with violence and aggression but can't get it up. Walter is a male fascist bastard.

The reader understands: this world is something which should rather not exist. Eating, devouring, farting, shitting, pissing, crazy desires, kinky sexuality, juices proliferating, and bodies gasping for breath, suffocating in saliva, sperm and urine. Obscene. Salamanders, snakes, spiders, bats, fish, eels. Walter's language is like a black cloud which envelopes everything in ultimate meaninglessness. There is no escape. One enormous Sadean obscenity. He is confronted in the end by a young black revolutionary with an AK 47 in his hands. The defender of women's rights to their bodies in his shining blackness. The ideal native son at last, even if fictional. Vincent rewritten. The novel ends with the word "Bang!"

Despite its topic and despite the fact that some women's groups read it in therapy sessions, the novel is not a success. Despite the fact that AF's review is enthusiastic and declares the novel a masterpiece of feminist literature, the sales figures are alarmingly low. Elise, by now accustomed to success, has a nervous breakdown. She lies in her bed and sees images: riderless horses, their maddened flanks and the saddle empty. It takes nine months before the earth becomes steady enough for her to leave her bed and attempt the first stumbling steps. She remembers less. The psychologist is certain that her breakdown was a late effect of her rape.

Charles was not allowed to read the novel. The prison librarian found it unsuitable for prison inmates. Bloody fucking pornography, if you ask me, he said. So Charles could not write a sneering review. Which would have been censored by the prison censor anyway. Had Charles not been sentenced to six years in jail or had Malva van Straaten written for the *Argus* or the *Sunday Times* instead of the *Vrye Weekblad* and *Die Burger*, Elise might have won the Booker Prize. At least. Bad luck. Putting your critic behind prison bars is not a good tactic.

Elise's mother, who had somehow heard about Elise's nervous breakdown, sent Elise baby dresses to remind her of her duty as a wife and mother. Elise's mother still sends her postcards depicting cats in various poses about once a week, with admonitions to remember her happy youth in the small house in Rondebosch.

Sweet memories.

That was not the end of Elise's career as a writer. She continued to write. Her next novel was a very avant-garde experimental piece of prose about her nervous breakdown. Her sales figures have never risen to the heights of *Sharing My Rug* or *You Have No Colour* again. But she hopes that she will one day be discovered by the academic critics. That may happen.

Vague suspicions

I DO REALISE THAT THE very fact that I am writing this letter to you makes me more rather than less a suspect. The very attempt to defend myself against rumours which are not even clearly formulated, and which I can therefore not really answer by clear and unambiguous denials, must make me seem guilty of whatever it is the rumours believe me to be guilty of. Only the guilty, you will argue, need to defend themselves even before they have been accused. Yet this present state of affairs when I am not accused of anything is far worse than any open accusation could be. The way people are shunning me does tell me quite clearly that they think I am guilty of the worst crime imaginable. Please, believe me: I have always supported the struggle of the people of South Africa to free themselves from the yoke of the apartheid regime. I am not saying this now because I am threatened by the wrath of the people or because I hope to retain my job as teacher in the New South Africa. I am simply trying to correct an impression which seems to be quite general although never formulated in so many words that I am one who in the past collaborated with the state.

I am deeply disturbed that this rumour about my past seems to be making the rounds. Yet I have never given anybody the slightest reason to suspect me of complicity with that evil system. As a child, already, I was the victim of the injustices of this system, when my father was forced to go to the Rand to earn money in the mines, and my mother, practically deserted by him and only rarely the recipient of a pitiable sum of money which he remitted through the mail, had to eke out a very meagre living from the tiny plot we were allotted in the most infertile part of the valley where we lived. While I escaped kwashiorkor and survived a number of infectious diseases, I grew up in a household that was not assured of even the minimal daily ration of mielies which I needed to grow into a healthy youngster. Like others of my age I had to hunt for rats, cane rats, birds and other small creatures of the veld to supplement the unhealthy diet I was given at home by my struggling mother. There were weeks and months when we did not know how to persuade the Jewish shopkeeper in the little town on the main road to the south to extend us some more credit, even though all our crops had failed in a particularly harsh drought. Even if I did not then understand how our daily deprivations were connected with something called apartheid, I did notice that the sons and daughters of the whites in the little town, the children of the shopkeepers, the policemen and the missionaries, never seemed to suffer from hunger, and that they were always well dressed, and did not have to wear clothes like mine, throwaway fourth-hand rags brought from the big cities by the mothers of other children working as maids there.

I do not know where and when I have said anything or, God forbid, done anything, which has set this unfortunate rumour into circulation. Should I indeed have said anything, it could only have been in a moment of anger or lack of concentration. But then even fervent comrades have in my presence voiced their exasperation with some elements of the Mass Democratic Movement without being ostracised for this momentary slip in loyalty, since everybody understands and accepts that a movement as large as ours cannot at all times satisfy the expectations of everybody, and that the behaviour of some of the representatives of the movement does indeed demand a critique. But I am sure that I indulged in such criticism even less than most of my friends, in fact there have been very few occasions in my life when I voiced such carefully phrased criticism, always attempting to be as objective as one can be under such circumstances.

Yet something must have happened which focused the eyes of my friends on me. How otherwise could there be such rumours about somebody like me who, from the days when I went to school at least, was a more and more convinced opponent of the apartheid regime? Admittedly, at first I believed it to be a very benevolent hand which took mine and led me to the old tin school-hut and taught me the relation between the sounds of my language and the weird white signs that my teacher drew on the blackboard in front of our schoolroom. But I soon learned from older schoolchildren in our village that the white school in the small town was a wonderwork of books, exercise books, pictures, films and educational toys, not to speak of sports fields and swimming pools. For the first time somebody clearly and unambiguously spelled out the difference in privilege and named the cause: apartheid. This same older scholar promised that once we had won the fight against apartheid we would join our white fellow students in their far more privileged school and partake of all the wonders there assembled. Since he also promised to return all our land to us which had been taken by the whites, and with the land a life of plenty in which we would not only no longer be hungry but be able to feast on meat and mielies to our heart's content, I was an immediate convert to the gospel of the opponents of apartheid.

It is true, I would not have been able to continue my schooling beyond Standard Three, not to speak of university, had there not been very helpful white hands who saw to it that I was given bursaries in proportion to my success at school, which indeed was spectacular. But even these gestures were seen by me very soon as a symptom of their guilt complex or as an attempt to co-opt me into their system, and while I had to take the money if I wanted to stay at school, I did not allow my principled opposition to the system to be deflected by such deeds of charity, which in any case were the least which the expropriators of my people's land could do to make up for their iniquities.

Taking into account my history of opposition and struggle, it seems absurd that some of my comrades seem to keep me under observation now. It is not as if I do not see the necessity for the greatest vigilance. This evil regime has succeeded in talking over and buying up so many of the people who we would have thought had every reason to support us in our struggle. They have even been able to subvert some of the comrades who were prepared to give their lives for the cause as soldiers of the Spear of the Nation and turn them into askaris, those truly despicable assassins of the leaders of the people. There are spies all over the place. No, vigilance is necessary. But me! It is ridiculous to think that anyone could suspect me of having sold my soul to the enemy!

I have even been in jail for the cause. When I finally managed to get a bursary for my university studies from some religious sponsor or other, I got involved in the Black Students' Society, was soon elected Honorary Treasurer and thus quickly came under the spotlight of the authorities. A boycott arranged by us in protest against some racist remarks made by a lecturer, saw me among the dozens of students roughly hauled from the campus and held under Section 29. The police must have seen that despite my involvement I was really a minor fish in the pond they were combing for freedom fighters and the leaders of the popular movements. So after seven weeks they dismissed me with a stern warning not to engage in what they called "subversive activities". Now it may have seemed strange that they let me go with two or three other equally minor fish when they continued to hold all the others for more than a year.

94

Whether this in the end contributed to the general atmosphere of distrust I do not know. Nobody at that time came out with any clear accusations, and nobody has since. On the contrary, much against my will, because I really wanted to complete my studies and the political work was very demanding and time-consuming, I was made acting chair of the Black Students' Society until such time as Comrade Chair would be released. It was after the release of these comrades that I was suddenly sidelined, not in a very obvious way, but sidelined nevertheless. I was told that I had held the fort admirably, but that I was in danger of being expelled from the university unless I completed at least two subjects this year and that I had better concentrate my attention on studying. This sounded strange, as usually the comrades argued that liberation should come before education, but since it coincided with what I wanted to do at that moment anyway, I agreed and did not accept any nominations to the executive that year.

I nearly did not get my bursary renewed that year because of the very mediocre record I had so far, but when I wrote to the secretary of the bursary scheme and pointed out that I had been in jail, the bursary was renewed with strict instructions that I attend to my studies and reduce my political involvement. It was at this time that I noticed that somebody was opening my mail. At first I thought this was a very crude attempt by the security police to find out what I was up to. But then I reflected that the security police would hardly be so inept as to leave such obvious traces of their handiwork. Then I suspected one of my comrades of attempting to steal money orders which I received every month from the bursary scheme. It was the custom in our hostel for one of us to go down to the mail room, fetch all the mail for the floor and distribute it to the students. If nobody was in a particular room, the letters would be left sticking in the crack of the door. It could really have been anybody tampering with my mail. But as I soon noticed, no money was ever removed from the letters. So somebody was interested in my correspondence. But who?

I could, of course, have reported this to the mail room or even to the Dean of Students. But both the official in the mail room and the Dean of Students were whites and members of the National Party, and any contact with them would have made my situation even more precarious. Several times I tried to spy on the person delivering the mail, but whenever I was anywhere around, my letters arrived with no visible sign of having been read. I never found out who was spying on me, but judging from my current situation, it is more than likely that my comrades even then suspected me of not being entirely trustworthy. Of course, I was enraged, but there was nothing I could do.

Things got worse when I was seen at the local police station. Now I had a very good reason to go there, there was in fact nothing I needed to hide, and therefore I did not make the least attempt to conceal my destination: I had lost a purse with twenty-five rand in it in a shop in town and I reported the loss to the police in the hope that whoever had found the money would return it to them. Twenty-five rand was a lot of money for me. I just could not afford to forget about the money without at least making an effort to retrieve it. As it happened I was called to the police station two weeks later and the purse and the money were returned to me. If my first visit to the police had gone unnoticed, this second visit definitely did not, since it was announced over the public address system during breakfast.

It was then that former friends started to avoid greeting me, crossed to the other side of the road when they saw me coming, stopped inviting me to parties or drinks. There was nothing about this which said: You are now totally ostracised in our community. It just happened, and as I was studying very hard at the time, it took me about four weeks really to understand what was happening. For a long time I resisted the paranoic impulse to interpret what was happening as a well-considered plot. While the conclusion that nobody wanted to have anything to do with me became more and more obvious, I was still prepared to believe in chance. My God, sometimes you are constantly in demand, you are popular, at other times people seem to have forgotten about your existence, and everything turns around some other person who is suddenly the centre of attention. It happens that way, and I knew that that is how things are.

Fortunately it was just before the final exams, I had little time for parties anyway, so I studied, although the niggling feeling that something was seriously wrong never left me.

It was during the next year, while I studied for my teacher's diploma, that I really became a case of full-blown paranoia. I began to see signs everywhere that my comrades had written me off. Now it is true that most of them had to do an extra year because of the year they spent in jail. I was thus surrounded mostly by students I did not know that well. But I lived that year in near total isolation, finding it more and more difficult to concentrate on my studies and completing the degree in a state of the utmost nervous excitation, which developed into something akin to a full-blown nervous breakdown in the week after the exam.

Returning to my home valley and my mother somewhat soothed the extreme tension under which I had been living. During these weeks I decided that the suspicion which must have arisen about me was so false and so obviously not in keeping with my character and education that, if I simply did nothing to attract any more attention, it would slowly die down, particularly as I would be in a completely different environment the next year as teacher in a school in a large town, totally removed from my comrades at university. Since I was normally quiet and reasonable, I was able to overcome my fear for the moment and actually looked forward to my employment as a teacher in the next year.

It soon became apparent, however, that the suspicions about my person must have preceded me to my new school, because from the first day my new colleagues refused to get involved with me to any degree except the barest minimum necessary to allow the teaching to go on as an activity in which we all shared. While the students at first were friendly, particularly the ones in Standard Six, within weeks I got the sensation that they all despised me and laughed at me behind my back. Only the headmaster remained friendly, but from some remarks I overheard in the staffroom he was considered to be on the side of the enemy.

It did not surprise me, therefore, that when the inevitable school boycott started towards June because the Department of Education had not sent the necessary school books, I was quietly but firmly excluded by colleagues and students. I was never informed of the actions they wanted to take the next day, and like the headmaster I found myself "out" of that inner circle which decided and planned these actions. While all the other teachers, even those who were not happy with the events of that winter, were virtually forced to take part in some capacity, either by helping with the painting of posters or by teaching alternative classes on the history of the struggle or by teaching protest poetry, I was left alone in a curious fashion.

My anxiety, of course, increased with the first act against "traitors" identified by the community. In many cases the evidence against the culprit was very slender – which I could see from my position as the outsider, but which those involved in these trials obviously could not. At first the reprisals were relatively harmless: offenders were given several strokes on their bare bottom or were paraded through the streets carrying posters saying: "I AM A POLICE SPY", and were spat upon by the community along the road. While I was horrified by such rough and ready justice, I would have preferred this kind of punishment, given that the community obviously did not trust me, to the ones which followed later.

Then the first person in our street, a sixteen-year-old member of a gang, who spent most of their time harassing young girls, was accused of feeding the police information which had led to the arrest of several leaders of the students. This youth was tried and found guilty of treason in the short span of ten minutes, and then bound, gagged and put inside a car tyre, doused with petrol, and set alight. After that I had no quiet moment in my life any more. The excruciating pain of this procedure stood before my eyes whatever I did: while I was trying to teach *Othello* in my matric class or the use of English idiom in my Standard Six one, I constantly smelled the fumes and the acrid smoke of this bonfire to justice. I could feel the petrol being poured over me, the match lit, the flames burning into my skin, the intense pain of the flames. Once I even collapsed in class under the most realistic impression of this ultimate punishment. I came to in the teachers' room, where one of my colleagues watched me intensely, and then said drily that I obviously could not cope with teaching, and that maybe I should try another, less stressful profession.

Had he found out about my attempts to get a post in one of the banks of the town, and my attempts to secure for myself with that job a house in a white suburb so as to flee the constant tension of life in the township? Perhaps his remark was entirely innocuous, the kind of thing an older teacher, inured to the hardships of teaching, would say to a younger colleague. Perhaps, I say.

I really went out of my mind when I came across three six-year-olds giving the "necklace" to the three-year-old brother of one of them in the streets as I walked home one afternoon from school. While they ran away frightened out of their wits, suddenly aware that this was no longer a game, I tried to kill the flames by throwing myself over the youngster. In the end I succeeded, but not before he had suffered considerable burns. I managed to phone an ambulance, and then I accompanied him to the hospital for blacks. There I collapsed, I lost consciousness, and when I came to, I was shaking all over and screaming wildly that I was innocent. Thank God, a harassed doctor gave me an injection which sent me off into a relaxed sleep, otherwise I do not know what I might have said.

The doctor was kind enough to give me a certificate stating that due to this extreme experience of violence I had had a minor nervous breakdown, and was unable to work until further notice. I sent this off to the headmaster explaining shortly what had happened, and received a get-well card from him. For two weeks I lay on my bed, unable to order my thoughts, constantly pursued by the image of a three-year-old child in flames. I not only sensed, I knew, that I would be the next victim of the popular displeasure with police spies and traitors. During those two weeks nobody visited me, and I did not go out, except to buy a few cans of food and beer. Most of the time I did not even bother to warm the food, but ate it out of the tin before flopping back on to the bed. Sometimes in the middle of the night I just caught myself wanting to run into the street and scream: OK, get me, I am a traitor. Kill me now. But make an end!

Slowly I became calmer. I told myself that if the community and my colleagues really suspected me, then they would have had ample opportunity to take their revenge. Although I was still visited by wild nightmares in which hordes of screaming people came running after me while I waded naked through knee-deep syrup, dreams from which I awoke sweating and yelling just before the first pursuer could touch me, I began to reason again, trying to sort out my predicament.

I have spent another week trying to write this letter. Often I had to go back to bed after one or two sentences. The attempt to pin down in exact words what has surrounded me as unspoken suspicion for many years has helped in the sense that I now know exactly what I am up against, but it was devastating in the sense that the longer I worked on formulating this letter, sentence by sentence, the more I realised how totally and irredeemably I was locked into this situation. I now understand that I will not be able to explain it to anybody.

Having reread this by now rather long letter, I have decided not to send it off to you. Even more clearly than when I began writing it, I now understand that this letter, if anything, incriminates me rather than excuses me. If the suspicion which I sense does exist and is not a figment of my paranoic imagination, then it must be strengthened by this attempt to exculpate myself. If, on the other hand, there never was any suspicion at all, and my isolation has other reasons than the ones which I suspect, then this letter will put questions into the minds of those who did not really question me before.

While you, as the chair of the Black Students' Society, would be the only one who could lift the suspicion which seems to surround me, if such suspicion does indeed exist, you would also be the one who would most effectively spread the suspicion which could arise out of this attempt to justify myself.

There is thus no way out of this situation but to go back to school tomorrow and simply go on teaching and living. As for the suspicion, I will have to deal with that entirely on my own. Perhaps it would even be best to destroy this letter, in case it should fall into the wrong hands.

Rain

U NTIL LATE THAT EVENING THE constant patter of rain, uniform, like the sound of a waterfall. Towards midnight the rain stopped. For a short while the slow drifting down of mist, the humidity trembling in the air, single drops falling from the branches of the trees – then it was quiet. The wet ground soaked up all sounds.

But she could not sleep. The silence was as disturbing as the constant splashing noise of the rain before. And the semi-tropical heat of Durban was oppressive, the air more like a warm fluid in which her body hung motionlessly, turning erratically from side to side. It was as if she was enveloped by a humid, sweaty cloth which penetrated all her pores. This was the first night in her new flat, the place she had bought after her mother died and she had sold the old house in which she had grown up. The death of her mother had suddenly opened up this enormous empty space in which her body now lived, touching nothing and nobody. In a way she liked this inconclusive and ambiguous existence. But she felt something creeping outside these walls, slimy and dirty, and she shuddered in revulsion at the thought that it might touch her one day, now that her mother was gone.

While her mother had been alive, her days had passed, the one much like the other, and as her years had passed her life had become less and less distinct to herself. Its outlines became blurred and washed out as if somebody had thrown water over a watercolour painting. For many years she had not known any strong pleasures which would have given her life a rhythm beyond that monotonous cycle of getting up, going to work, and returning home to an evening of TV and going to bed again. There must have been a time when life was nearer to her body than now, but in the years in between she had withdrawn from her body and attended to what seemed more important matters. She talked to the people she met in the office or when she went shopping, she saw the things that happened around her, but she never had a strong desire to come near them, nothing that happened was related to her life in any way.

She could hardly remember the excitements of her girlhood, the new dresses on her birthdays and at Christmas, the occasional party to which she had been allowed to go, although she always had to be home before twelve.

She could hardly remember the excitement of her schooldays, the stolen minutes in the park with that boyfriend of hers before she had to ride home on the bus, the rush of pleasure when she had finally kissed Alfons on the lips, her first and her last kiss, and the sudden pain when the boy who was considered the most desirable in her class suddenly no longer looked at her. Just simply ignored her. But she hardly remembered the pain of that discovery, although in a way she knew that it had been traumatic. She had locked herself in her room every afternoon and cried. It all seemed so distant and childish now in its innocence and futility.

As she turned over on her bed she tried to think about her job, but tomorrow was Saturday, and the weekend made all the unimportant decisions of her secretarial everyday seem so distant and unreal, that they were unable to erase the image of that kiss. That kiss now seemed to her disgusting, and Alfons a repulsive creep, but still she held on to this moment when two wet lips met and clung to each other, as if drinking the elixir of life.

In the end she decided to get up and take a shower. She went to the window and pushed aside the heavy dark-blue curtains and the light transparent gauze, and opened the side window wide. But the air outside was as hot and humid as the air in her room. The park in front of her window was in total darkness, and the glass of the window was like a dark basin of water on a calm, windless day. There was nothing to see except this warm, humid darkness. She wondered whether there were hoboes sleeping in the park. She saw them each morning lying on the benches in the sun. There were men, mostly older men, with the ravaged features of the heavy drinker, their faces ruddy from the sun. There was something animal-like in the way they lay on the benches, but it reminded her of the moth-eaten, sad-looking animals of the zoo rather than the wild animals she had once seen when she went to Umfolozi with her mother. The women were dirty, and she imagined them sleeping with the men in the park, without undressing, shamelessly in public.

She went across into the bathroom, switched on the light, took off her nightgown and started to shower. The cool water turned up full pierced her skin like little needles. When she stepped out of the shower, she cleaned the full-length mirror with her towel, and suddenly had the feeling of being nearer to herself than ever before, although the image she saw in the mirror was totally foreign: that body was not her body, surely. As her hands slid over her naked body she saw this strange woman stroking herself in the mirror and looking out of the mirror at her in a shameless way, so that she felt exposed, as if somebody had asked her to pose for a nude photograph. And yet at the same time she liked being looked at and looking, a woman and her body looking at another woman and her body, she and the mirror image, her body in a trancelike state of well-being. It was a fascination with the gaze which travelled over her skin like a tickling feather. She had always believed what the uninterested looks of men had made her believe: that her body was not worth looking at, if not ugly. But now she was suddenly one with the body she felt under her hands, though not with the strange body she saw in the mirror, nor with its eyes on her.

She switched off the light and walked back into the bedroom, still naked, and felt the warm, sticky air flowing over her body, as her body moved in the darkness. The darkness filled the room like a heavy fluid. There was a restless tenderness in her but it lacked any direction. She felt as if she was expanding in all directions, as if her fingers could touch the horizon through the window. She had an unclear, flowing image of herself, as if she had no boundaries. But she did not know what to do about the emotion. She could not even imagine a man who could become the goal of that unfocused emotion. No, not a woman either. She smiled at that thought: not even that woman in her mirror. And yet her tenderness reached out into the darkness of the night searching. It was like something which had been dead and called back to life but did not know how to adapt to the new situation which had grown over the years when it was dead. This ghost of an emotion wandered about, it was like a mere shadow in the general darkness of the room. Yet it had a powerful, unusual sensuality, it searched for flesh and pulsating blood, for the softness of skin and hair, as she was moving aimlessly and without shame through her darkened room.

As she sat on the carpet, she suddenly remembered Charles, how she had surprised him on the toilet one day, she must have been twelve or thirteen, when she had been visiting his younger sister Hilda, who was then her best friend. He had forgotten to lock the toilet, and was sitting there with his red head on the toilet, pumping his thing between his legs, and as she opened the door this white stuff had spurted out all over the tiles, and he got even redder in his face. She felt herself go tense in all her muscles and red all over, and a curious loathing had overcome her, while she stood in the open door for an endless moment gazing at this nauseating event, until she caught herself and banged the door behind her. From that day on Charles could never look her in the eyes, and always found an excuse to disappear when she came to visit.

At that moment she did not understand at all what had happened, but that night when she was in bed, she had suddenly grasped the meaning of that act, and she found that the nausea was now mixed with a shrill excitement which she could not explain to herself. While she pictured again before her mind what she had seen, she felt how her body tensed and eased rhythmically with the movement of Charles's hand in her memory. Finally she had fallen into an exhausting sleep.

When her mother had gone out the next day, Harris, her dog was sleeping in the room where she studied, and looking at him she recognised the thing between his legs for what it was. She had never before looked at it consciously. She had always seen the dog as a living thing which was there as her plaything, but she had never considered it as something which had a sex. Of course, she knew that dogs were male and bitches were female, just as she knew that boys were male and girls female. But she had never, until she surprised Charles, thought of boys and girls as being endowed with sex either. She got up and knelt beside the dog, and playfully pushed back the hairy skin under which she saw the scarlet tip of the penis. Thinking of Charles she began to rub the skin forward and backward, the hair on the dog's back began to stand up straight, and when the strong-smelling whitish liquid came, she was startled, and suddenly afraid. She felt as if she was rolling in mud and rubbish with her naked body, yet that thought, too, gave her an immense pleasure, as if she had waited all her life, which had been so pure and clean, for this moment of abandoning all the rules of her mother's puritan cleanliness. She chased out the dog and quickly tried to scrub the carpet without making it too wet, but the strong smell remained for many days.

She always wondered why her mother had not smelled it.

She had not remembered this for years, and she did not know why she remembered it tonight, her first night on her own, in her own flat. She sat on the carpet and tried to get rid of the image. She tried not to think of Charles or the dog, but she did not succeed, however much she tried, she felt herself in the unbreakable grip of a fascination. But then the sudden fear she had felt many years ago overcame her like an enormous wave and bowled her over, until she lay shaking on the floor, gibbering, and calling for mama. Her whole body shook convulsively, while she screamed and howled and whimpered. For minutes she lost control over her body, and her body threw her around on the floor and against the table, the chairs, the wall. After one last spasm she collapsed on her stomach and kept on lying motionless for a long time. Then she got up.

She felt curiously drained, as if she had a sudden fever, her head was empty and the blood hammered in her temples. She went back to bed, but she could not sleep. She slowly closed her eyes and slowly opened them again. She rolled up in her darkness and could not understand what had happened to her then, in her room with the dog, or now, in this night. With open eyes she stared at the ceiling. Once when she closed her eyes she again had this vision of her dog, Harris, in her room, and she could actually smell his strong dog smell. She rolled restlessly on her bed for a few more hours. She had the impression that something inside her, some fine vessel, had broken in the violence of her uncontrolled body, and that she was bleeding to death, and that if she had had the feeling before that her life had been empty, she now had the feeling that it was defiled and worthless and shabby. She wished for the darkness to go away, but she did not hope that her emptiness would now ever leave her again. Finally there was a faint light with the slightest flush of a rosy colour in her window. She went to the window and closed the gauze curtain and looked out over the park which slowly changed from dark and black clumps into green trees and grass, and she saw one of the hoboes lying on the bench under the huge flame tree, until there was a sudden fanfare of light as the sun rose over the horizon and blotted out all things in its harsh brilliance.

Little girls must listen to their parents or feel the rod

MY ROOM WAS IN FLAMES. The flames danced all around me. I woke up, sweating and with my heart beating wildly, and unable to move. My scream was still resounding in my ears, but nobody else seemed to have heard me in the large house with the thick walls and solid doors. Only the frogs piped outside the window in their high-pitched voices. In the moment I woke up I started to scream and writhe on my bed, but nothing I did was able to loosen my hands or my feet. I could not move. I discovered that I had been nailed to the bed with huge iron nails which pierced my hands and my feet, like in the pictures I had seen of Jesus on the cross, only that my hands and feet had been stretched out in the form of an x to the wooden sides of the bed. While I continued to scream my mother appeared in the flames and she said solemnly: If you don't listen, you must be punished. Then her face disappeared, and was replaced by the furious face of my father, who shouted: You must learn to obey! To do what you are told to do!

But, dear mother, I screamed, have I not always done what you told me to do?

And, dear father, I shouted, have I not been the most obedient, good little girl of my dear father all the time?

Girls who tell lies, said my father sadly, must burn in hell!

You have been very naughty, said my mother in tears. Now nobody can save you any more. Girls who are naughty must burn in hell.

But, I wanted to say.

No buts, shouted my father and hit me with his cane over my bare legs. Children should be seen, not heard. Children should not argue with their father. No buts!

But, I wanted to say, I was naughty because.

No because, shouted my mother, and took the cane from my father and hit me with the cane over my hands. You were very naughty, you have brought horrible shame on this family. You were nasty, dirty, bad. And you were telling lies.

But, I thought, but did not say any more, I have only done what you wanted me to do, daddy. I have been your obedient little girl all the time. I have been obedient to you in the same way that you told me you had to be obedient to your father. I did everything, everything.

You are nasty, shouted my mother. You are bad, through and through. Now, see what you have done to your poor father. Shameful! He can no longer show his face anywhere because of your lies.

That was why the room was full of flames and the flames were all over my body, and my body was nailed to the bed, and I was ashamed and wanted to close my eyes so that I would no longer see my shameful body as it was lying on the bed, but my mother forced my eyes open with her hard fingers, and I had to see my dirty body as it was stretched out on the bed.

My mother pointed to a place between my legs and shouted, see, see, see, there she has fouled her bed. Do you see the stain? The whore's stain!

I could not see the stain, but I could feel the wetness.

Here I am, sobbed my mother, sick, so sick that I had to go to hospital and have an operation, and I did not even know whether

I would live, and hardly am I out of my door, you go and drag your father into your bed. And you not even ten years old.

I was crying. Because it was not true. I did not drag my father into my bed. That was the last thing I wanted.

But I know you, you slut! My mother shouted. Always playing with boys. Always lifting up your skirts. Always rolling in the dirt. Always telling smutty stories and lies about your parents.

Yes, said my father, remember when I caught you in the tool shed with Hannes, and he took off his pants. And you were showing him your nasty belly button. I caught you then. That's what you are like. You are bad, through and through. I caught you then, didn't I, and he laughed his slimy, tittering kind of laughter, until he started to choke. Always holier than thou, and then she slinks off into the tool shed with a boy.

I was crying, because I knew that I was bad through and through, and that he had caught us in the tool shed while we were looking at our bellies where one is not supposed to look. But he was looking too, when he hit us on our naked behinds.

You see, you are a whore, my mother shouted. And you not even ten years old. Oh God, what is to become of you. Here I am, sick, so sick that I had to go to hospital and have an operation, and I am probably going to die, and the excitement does not help at all, and you go and drag your father into your bed. You little slut.

I was crying, because I knew that I was bad through and through, and that I had done something horrible which could never be made good again, and that therefore I had to die and go to hell, and the flames of hell were around me already, all over my body, and the nails were holding me down on my bed, and the devils would come dancing round my bed and throw glowing coals on my belly, and my legs wide open for the fire to come in to burn out my insides.

Asking your father to bathe you! You witch! When you never liked me to bathe you because, you said, you were now old enough to wash yourself! What a cheap trick, and of course, your poor father fell for it. What a cheap trick, you little whore!

I was crying, because I burned in hell, and because this was all so unfair, and I had not asked my father to wash me, because when my mother had gone off to hospital, and I wanted to go to bed and went to the bathroom, he just came with me and said, tonight I am going to wash my little princess in champagne and he laughed his tittering, high-pitched laugh, and I blushed and did not know what to say to him at all. Anyway he was just sitting there and leering at me while I undressed. And then he started to feel me all over, while pretending to wash me with his hands and soap.

But the worst, said my father, is that she just couldn't keep her mouth shut, that she had to go and spread all these lies about me, and so we are going to be called to the magistrate next week, and all because of you we are going to jail, maybe, and your mother so sick that she had to go to hospital and have an operation, and that is why you are going to burn in everlasting fire and the devil will roast you day and night, to burn all that badness out of you.

And then crawling into my bed with him, naked little whore! Has one ever seen the like? Trying to play mummy with daddy and making him all eager until he falls for you, you dirty little slut!

I was crying and crying, because this was all so unfair, as I had not wanted to go to bed with him at all, but he grabbed me and towelled me, and took me on his arm, all without clothes to the big bedroom where he and my mother are sleeping together, but I don't think they really sleep together, because they did not have any babies for a very long time, and I know that you get babies when you sleep together, and he put me on the bed and took off all his clothes, and I was very frightened and did not know what to do, because I wondered whether I was going to have a baby.

I am sure you enjoyed it, too, she shouted. And the flames were all over the bed, and my body, and the walls and table, and all my room was burning, and I could not breathe any more because of the smoke and the flames, and I gagged and nearly stopped breathing.

I am sure you enjoyed it, you little whore, she shouted, and she began to beat me with my father's cane on the belly, and I screamed in pain and then I cried, because I had not enjoyed it at all, it hurt like hellfire even then, and I felt as if my belly was going to burst and split, and blood would run out of me, and when he had finished, I was crying, and he said, you enjoyed that, didn't you, my sweet little princess, and I nodded, and I still cried, but I had not enjoyed it at all, and when I had finished crying, there was blood on the sheets, where he had pushed his thing into my belly, and I was very sore, and I could not sleep all night, because I was afraid that he would do this again. So some time during the night I crawled out of his bed, and he kept on snoring, and I went to my room and locked myself in.

And I screamed. And screamed. And screamed. But nobody seemed to hear me, there were only the voices of my parents in the room, and I could not even see their bodies and their heads any more, there were just these voices that condemned me to hell and to this burning fire.

But in the morning before I got up to go to school he came and banged on my door, and when I did not open, he got an axe and broke open the door, and he did it again with me, and then every day, until my mother came back from hospital, and then that night, when he thought she was asleep he came again, and the noise must have awakened her, because as he was on me she came in, and saw the two of us on my bed, and that is when the flames started to burn in this room, and everything started to go terribly wrong with all of us, and I don't see how I could have stopped him from doing what he did. So, how can it be my fault, all this dirt, and he is still here, all naked with his pot belly, how I hate him.

And I could see the devils climbing in through the window,

with their long tails hanging down between their legs, and they were laughing as they took their black forks and stuck them into my belly. And the devils all looked like daddy and mummy, and they laughed and danced around my bed in the flames, and one of them was waving a pistol in his hand, and was shooting the other, until she fell down on the floor, and then he put the pistol in his own mouth, and shot himself, and fell down, and the fire of hell was all over the place. And they laughed like hell, and while they were lying on the floor as if they were dead, they also danced around in the room and laughed, so that I wanted to cover my ears with my hands, but my hands were nailed down on the bed. And so I had to listen to their dirty talk about piss and fuck and suck and dicks and cunts and holes and fingers and buds and I was blushing and sweating, and I hated them and I was roasting in the fire, and I didn't even have tears any more, it was that hot in the room, and my voice had evaporated and I could not talk any more, not even croak.

And so as the house burns to the ground, there is a lot of noise now outside, and the sirens of the police and the firemen, but I think they are coming too late as always. They never get it, they are just too stupid to notice anything until it is too late, and I think I will burn in the fires of hell for ever although I have always been a good little girl and always did what I was told to do, except that day when my father caught us in the tool shed without our clothes on.

Top secret: cannibalism

THE MARKS WHICH HUMAN TEETH make in human flesh, the hole which is created by this absurd hunger, seems to be an emptiness that is impossible to observe. Yet it is this very emptiness and absence, the impossibility of finding any evidence, which grips the collective imagination of millions. This emptiness between the imaginary bite-marks erupts in newspapers and on TV programmes, in bars and on the beach, in offices and workplaces. This empty space, never observed, attracts stories in all the places where people meet so as to make itself real. Tales like this can only be written down because they encircle such an absence: the signs of a secret horror parade on the white page which nevertheless remains empty, the story unfolds its imaginary path, yet never arrives anywhere.

The disquieting rumours reached me everywhere, whispering through the banana leaves of the semi-tropical slums, rattling the rusting tin roofs of the peri-urban sprawl, rustling in the endless sugar-cane fields, throwing up sand in the quiet seaside holiday resorts of the north and the south coasts, and threatening the third-rate Disneyland of the tourist trade in Durban, the largest harbour town of the province. Somewhere in the mud of the mangroves near the slimy waters of Richards Bay, the coal harbour in the north, the severed hand of a white soldier was supposed to have turned up. In the dry dune forest between a sugar farm and the sea near Mtunzini an old black servant was said to have found the sawed-off cranium of an unidentified human being. Unverifiable reports of human toes and fingers having been found in the soups or the stews of five-star hotels reached me while I was crawling through the thorn bushes of the game reserves to find the remains of a game warden, who, according to reports, had been braaied near the junction of the White and the Black Umfolozi. But when we reached there, the site was two metres under the brown swirling waters of the river, and any trace presumably washed down into the Indian Ocean.

Finally the whole province began to smell of the rotting meat of the human victims of this elusive monster, which was reported to have struck at the most distant locations from the sea to the towering, snowclad mountains of the interior, sometimes hundreds of kilometres apart, and even at the same time. But wherever I went, the monster was no longer to be found. Not that there were no corpses: more human bodies turned up in the drawers of mortuaries than I could investigate.

An eleven-year-old, who was spending the night with a friend, was found with sjambok-marks all over his skinny body, reportedly left for dead by the monster who had abducted him. It was said that the monster had already cut the head off the body, when it was disturbed by the men of the village. When I investigated, however, it seemed that the boy and his brother had been involved in a school boycott and that his attackers were three community councillors.

That's the problem with rumours: they proliferate, they acquire new details with every retelling, and when you follow them up, there is always just nothing, or nearly nothing, which is worse, because the trace of reality in all its ambiguity convinces you that there is some kind of solid nucleus to all this talking and talking. That is why I decided to write this down: after sorting all the fictions from the few facts, I believed I might discover the clue that has become obscured in the endless telling and retelling of people talking and whispering, seducing the fickle brain into believing what is not, into seeing what is only an uncertain shape in the mist and cloud and steam of the spoken words.

Of course, in the beginning, I felt proud, when Major General Johann Coetsee singled me out to be the one to investigate this disturbing phenomenon.

Pieter, he said, you are the person to look into this, although it may be more than you can handle. There are some indications which point to somebody very powerful being involved in this. That is why this thing is top secret. From here on you are on your own. I know I can rely on you.

Top secret, as I soon found out, was a huge joke: everybody, I mean everybody from Ndumu to the Transkei coast and from Durban to Mont-aux-Sources was talking about nothing else, and I just needed to enter any bar to be told without even asking the latest horror story: a two-year-old girl baked in bread-dough in Dukuduku Forest or a human sausage factory discovered in a remote kloof on the Swazi border.

Yet the stories were totally inaccessible: for whenever I finally arrived in the Dukuduku Forest or in that remote kloof on the Swazi border, nobody had the faintest idea what I was talking about, although they had heard about these atrocities, of course – wasn't there this story about the grandmother and her two granddaughters, whose dismembered parts had been discovered in a chimney, well salted and spiced, ready to be smoked, must have been somewhere near the Transkei border.

While the descriptions were often very vague – I mean, the Transkei border is long – sometimes, as in the case of the house and the oven in the Dukuduku Forest, they were quite detailed. So, while the game ranger I had questioned shook his head unbelievingly, I set out along the dirt road which corresponded exactly to the description my source in Howick had given me. The dense forest on the left, nearly impenetrable, a subtropical green wall, the open brush on the right with single trees was exactly as described. As I was driving further a brown eagle with long feathers rising from his crown laboriously lifted himself from one of the withered tree skeletons, uttering a harsh scream. Later the forest closed in from both sides and the shrill high-pitched noise of the Christmas beetles filled my ears with rage. Just as I had been told, the road suddenly petered out into a wet patch of open grassland. What I couldn't see at first was the wooden hut with the baking oven which was supposed to stand on the other side of the grass at the edge of the forest.

I got out of the car and skirted the marshy grassland, and was on the point of giving up when I noticed the faint trace of a former path, now nearly invisible under a thicket of lianas, grass and bushes. I went back to the car, fetched a panga and began hacking my way into the thicket. Surprisingly, about ten metres into the bush the undergrowth started to clear and the mighty trunks of large trees rose nearly unhindered from the ground, which was covered in decaying leaves. By now the path was no longer visible, but to my right a round earthen form came into view among the trees. At first it looked like an enormous anthill. As I came nearer, I recognised the old-fashioned baking oven which corresponded exactly to the description I had been given. But the hut had collapsed and all that remained was a rotting heap of old planks and wooden posts, lying in a shambles.

In the sudden silence the call of an emerald cuckoo – *meitjie meitjie meitjie* – reminded me of my purpose and I began to scratch around in the oven. But whoever had been baking here had left very long ago. Except for the black soot in the large gaping hole of the oven there was now no sign that this structure had ever been used. Neither did I uncover anything unusual among the planks and posts of the collapsed hut. I was about to make my way back to the car when I saw a little bone lying half-covered by one of the planks. It must have been a bone from the finger, and comparing it to my own fingers, I guessed that it was a child's. That is when I began to work like a man possessed, shifting every single rotting plank of the hut, sweating in the intense heat of the afternoon, and trembling with fatigue and excited anticipation in the incessant noise of the Christmas beetles, which had resumed their concert. After six hours of labour, and exhausted by the physical exertion, I collapsed next to the oven, with nothing more to show than that single bone.

While my hands dug idly into the ground, they suddenly came up with a ring. After some polishing, the ring revealed an inscription: Betty 9 March 1928. The next day I came back with a spade and a sieve and for twelve hours dug over the entire ground underneath the hut and around the oven. Not much more showed up: a rusty drinking mug with chipped enamel, a stainless-steel knife, a small blue enamel pot with tiny white spots.

The forensic laboratory identified the bone as the finger-bone of a small child about two years of age, but insisted that it must have lain in the ground for more than forty years. The police were unable to trace the present or previous owner of the decayed structure. So: nothing, unless this was the last sign of a murder committed some forty years ago. But the rumours spoke about a man-eater who was on the prowl now.

No real evidence, however. As I scribbled notebooks full of stories as I heard them, and kept accurate reports on my researches in the most remote corners of the province, I began to realise that all this writing seemed to point to an absence: but absences do exist as names, and this one definitely made an impact on the lives of people.

For one moment, however, in a remote kloof on the dangerous mountain road between Mkuzi and Ndumu on the Swazi border, I believed I had found incontrovertible evidence of the reality of the man-eater. After making my way along the wet and slippery road to the village that had been pointed out to me, I spent two hours talking to the headman through an interpreter. He had no knowledge of the cannibalist feast which was supposed to have taken place not more than five kilometres from his home, but made vague references to a Tsonga tribe living further north who he said were ritually slaughtering people every year just before the rainy seasons started. (A later investigation of that tribe showed that they were living off the fish of the Pongola River, and there was no evidence whatsoever that they now were or in the past ever had been cannibals.)

What we found in the kloof, next to a small waterfall under the heavy canopy of the riverine forest, was horrific enough: fifteen men, women and children, brutally hacked to death, many of them dismembered as if in preparation for cooking them, their stomachs bloated and decomposing, flies everywhere. The stench was noticeable long before we reached the scene, and as we came round the exposed rocks into this idyllic little opening it became so overpowering, the sight so revolting, that I began to vomit until only yellow gall and bitter white fluid filled my mouth, still retching, but unable to vomit any more.

The police, whom we called immediately, established what we had understood soon enough: this was the scene of a butchery but not the scene of an inhuman meal. It seemed that all the murdered belonged to a family of migrant workers, whose three bread-winners had come home for a funeral, and who were suspected by the authorities of being members of the African National Congress. Who exactly was responsible for the murder was never established, but many fingers pointed to the headman of that little village we had just visited, who was known to be an ardent follower of Inkatha.

While the evidence remained elusive the image of the cannibal became clearer and clearer. We were dealing with a man who was superhumanly strong. Some of those claiming to be eyewitnesses who had escaped from one of the ritual slaughters said that he could snap the neck of a grown man with his bare hand: like an axe it descended on the victim, followed by a loud crack, a scream stopped halfway in its utterance, and then silence. He would then cut the throat of his victim with a huge butcher's knife, his green eyes aglow.

He was also supposed to have roasted the livers and hearts of his victims, while he cooked arms and legs in a huge pot. Other reports stated that he had a huge paraffin fridge on the back of his van, like the ones fishermen use when they go on their annual holidays in Natal, and that he stowed the cleaned and dismembered bodies in this fridge.

At the end of the eight months which I spent in Natal I had fifty-eight rather detailed reports on such slaughters – not counting the vague rumours I could pick up at any bar in the country – but very little in concrete evidence and no idea who the killer, if he existed, could be.

We dream of these things in order to explain the horror we feel, to give it shape, but the true shape of the horror escapes us all the time. The evidence we had was singularly inconclusive. It is true, severed limbs or heads would be found again and again in abandoned houses, in destroyed shacks, in indigenous forests, and once on the beach of a small holiday village on the south coast. But in most cases these could be traced to the civil war between the ANC and Inkatha and in several cases the killers were even brought to court, although that was rare. While some of the human remains were in the end unaccounted for, that did not necessarily connect them to the mysterious cannibal.

So why did I still believe in his existence? Clear, logical, investigative, criminalist thinking should have convinced me that if the cannibal was not a huge hoax invented by somebody to distract our attention from something worse going on in Natal, it was a myth sprung from the collective mind of the people. Yet the cannibal was far too real for either of these hypotheses to be true. Despite my inconclusive hunt I became more and more convinced of his existence. No logic, no ever-extending network of lianas, can come to grips with the discontinuity and fictionality of real existence, the sheer genius of this silence which never gives itself and its desire away.

So I was quite disappointed when Major General Johann Coetsee recalled me from Natal, and from the elusive chase for what appeared to be a phantom. While I had to give up driving from suspect locality to suspect locality, my mind has never ceased to explore the dark semi-tropical rainforests of Natal and the endless sugar-fields, the riverine forests and the thornveld, the rural settlements and the urban slums, the back alleys around the harbour and the beach cottages of the holiday resorts. Having handed in my four-wheel drive, I now trace the progress of the cannibal on paper. One thing is certain: he must have been very mobile and he must have used a vehicle that can reach even the most uncharted corner of this province over paths where the normal family car would get hopelessly bogged down. For some time I even wondered whether he had used a helicopter, but then decided that that would have been too conspicuous.

Writing is waiting, writing is hope, writing is using up paper and ballpoints. But there can be no history and no truth without writing. Yet even in the written letters the truth seems to be hidden, not easily seen. There is a lapse of attention when I seem to have grasped the meaning, a lapse which has nothing to do with the darker memory of the language. I felt as if I had collected the scattered bones of the child-God eaten by us all, blood dripping from our lips, in the little notebooks in which I jotted down all the reports I heard and followed up. As I go through all my notes of the last two years, the clue seems to elude me, and all the commentary I wrote to remind me of possible pointers to the truth which flashed through my mind, as I read and reread the hastily scribbled field notes of my expeditions into the interior of this strange province, does not make the notes any clearer. On the contrary, like the rumour, which this writing attempted to dispel, the commentary proliferates and envelopes the few facts with more and more speculation. Of course, the commentary is necessary, because the few facts that remain are singularly silent; they may be clues, but they don't speak. I do not know what is worse: the dismembered facts which do not make sense or the commentary which attempts to make sense out of them but in doing so obliterates the facts. Sometimes I feel I am a victim of the rebellion of the words: they grow and grow and any sense and utterance there may have been has been overgrown by weeds long ago.

Unisex

W E TALK AND WE TELL stories, and we say: I did that or that happened to me. I am merely telling you a story, a little story about myself. It is not about witches and mothers, and it is not about half-natural little creatures like dwarves and giants which populate the lands beyond the boundary of fairy tales, there where we are no longer simply serious, but deadly serious, where we are not satisfied unless we push the witch into the pre-heated oven and turn the dial to full steam. No, this is a story about me, and when you have read the story you might want to switch on your own oven, although I would prefer it if you would find another solution to your problems. So, instead of asking me whether the story is more or less true, perhaps you should just accept that the story exists, in the same way that you accept Snow White exists. And instead of asking whether "I" exist who tell the story, and how you can get hold of me and roast me in your best Sunday anger, it may be more useful to ask me where it begins and where it ends, and what the boundaries are that limit that "I", and I would not be surprised if you discover that such borders not only cut through me when I tell this story, but also through you when you read it, and that may be the very reason why you want to switch on the oven.

The problem with your anger, or one of the problems with it, is that I am double: there is one I who tells the story, and another I about whom the story is told. Your rage attempts to put into one what may fall apart into a puzzle of potentialities, a situation where one obsession no longer knows what goes on in another region of your body. And that maybe is something which that superior central identity thing, your I or ego, cannot stomach: Revolution! Madness! Pervert! Well, you are free to torture your vocabulary, but you are not free not to know. That is why you are still reading. If your rage were genuine you would put down the book now and burn it, since you might find it difficult to burn me. But it is not, since you want to find out whether, despite your denials, there is not something like me in you too. And whether the written text will tell you something you have never yet known or experienced.

The problem, of course, is that you don't know, and never can, or at least not until it is too late. Because wherever there is an area of silence, there is an area of ambiguity, undecidability. It slips through all controls and knows all the ruses of appearing perfectly normal, sometimes so perfect that it becomes suspicious in its normality. And there are the censors, yes, the ones inside, and the ones outside, and each attempts to be more efficient than the other, but, oh dear, they are so stupid, they always ban the wrong things, watching their feeble erections instead of the aborted birth of an unusual idea in their reverberating hollow heads. You can't trust them! They are no defence whatsoever.

If you were to meet me, I can assure you, you would not confuse me with either the one who tells this story or the one whose story is told here. I look totally different from the narrator or the main character of this story, so don't even try to identify me. To give you an idea: every morning punctually at eight thirty I enter my office, my hair trimmed in exactly the way you would expect of a servant of this government, my tie is beautifully discreet, my double-breasted suit conforms to all the norms for the well-dressed bureaucrat. I do not stick out, you could easily confuse me with a few hundred other bureaucrats in the same building. I greet my secretary jovially, I even indicate to her playfully that I have an erotic interest in her, in such a manner, of course, that she takes it as a flirtatious joke, yet as a compliment to her beauty, and in the manner of all the other office patriarchs I graciously let her serve me a coffee while I settle down to the morning newspaper in preparation for my day's routine. I am perfectly capable of playing the role of the man, the straight ou, the guy you can take for a drink to the bar, the guy you respect, who has just the right amount of aggression to make his way upwards in the hierarchies of bureaucracy without ever blocking his own way by being wrong-headed or unreasonable.

We are all so beautifully one, because we are all two or three or many. We are one, because the other one or two or many which we are trying not to be provide the boundary of the fairy tale which we may never enter. So there is already this threefold division of this I who tells a story about me, and myself as my colleagues and friends know me, with whom I go to have a drink after office hours, and take an occasional afternoon off to watch cricket. Now, I may be wrong, but when I hear them laugh at certain jokes in the bar, or when they watch these wonderfully athletic young men on the cricket pitch with hungry eyes, I am pretty sure that they are as multiple and confused as I am, the only difference is that they hold on with such vigour to that oneness that they feel themselves threatened by anyone who has let his unity slide into confusing duplicity. That, of course, is the reason why I have to be aware of myself constantly, why I have to play my role so perfectly in the office: one mistake, one slip of the mask, one ambiguous movement of my legs, my hands or my bum, one glimpse of my multiplicity, and they would all hunt me to the end of their world and beyond, even into fairy-tale land where one can make roast meat out of witches and monsters.

It was when I visited a distant aunt, I must have been about fifteen then, that I suddenly saw this image arising out of a deep forgetting which had lasted many years. My aunt had given me the room of my cousin, who was absent for the time of the vacation. As I undressed that first evening away from home, there was this sudden sensation on my skin, all over my body, the softness and movement of a dress which I had worn as a child of three when I had wanted to be a girl: at that time my mother, a widow, had kept me in dresses until just before I had to go to school. As I stood there in the room of my cousin at the age of fifteen, naked, I was suddenly that little girl-boy again in the skin of that fantasy, the billowing, fluttering and caressing girl's dress, and I didn't understand now, as I had not then, why I could not be a girl if I really wanted to, although I couldn't say why I wanted it. For my three-year-old self, the scene ended in tears, in this hopeless knowledge that it was an image from which I was to be excluded for ever. Before I went to school my hair was cut short, and new school clothes had to be bought. I very reluctantly took leave of my girl-person and learnt very quickly and the hard way not to be a sissy but what was called a real boy. My infancy had come to an end.

There were no images going further back than that at the age of three to suggest why at that age I wanted to be a girl, wanted to wear dresses. Because wearing a dress was a body experience, a desire, not merely a decision of my mother. But that desire was shrouded in amnesia. This first trace must have been inscribed outside my presence, before I was there, before I was a person having memories. I have tried in vain to recognise this first thing, that cause, that initial scene. Perhaps there is no first thing, no initial scene, no real cause.

So, as I was standing there in the room of my cousin, undressed, ready to go to bed, I suddenly wanted to return to that scene. I had this bodily sensation of wearing dresses, this precise and yet diffuse image of myself in a dress. Stripped bare, the event had already occurred: I had changed in a way which imbued me with a new certainty about myself. What I experienced, if I may use such paradoxical language, was a femininity dating from a time when there were no women, a femininity which I am now acting out with such accomplishment. Yet without the veil of clothes I would not have been able to uphold the truth of the person who I knew I was. It is through concealment that meaning is created. With my clothes removed I could see like any other woman that I was much too fat here and too thin there, my breasts diminutively small, my legs too hairy, my waistline invisible. I locked the door of the bedroom, although there was little chance that my aunt would come this late at night into my room, opened the wardrobe of my cousin, which, though depleted by the clothes she had taken with her on her holiday, contained some of her party dresses, underwear, bras, nylon stockings, and even a blonde wig with long, shiny, flowing hair.

A woman is not something biological or natural, the existence or non-existence of certain body parts which stick out or are invisible, the gentle fold of flesh which surrounds the secret: a woman is a work of art created in clothing, obliterating and hiding the parts of the body which do not conform to the ideal of a woman. Stripped bare, I was a biological misfit with appendages which contradicted my identity; in men's clothes I was an actor performing in a role that did not really correspond to me in any way, though I could do a creditable imitation of that maleness. It was only now that the black silk slip of my cousin began to hide the signs of my biological identity that I began to come near to a well-being which I had not known for a long time. I put on the support bra which needed little further padding, I pulled up the nylon stockings, and put on the blonde wig. As I turned my head in front of the mirror, this new hair felt like a weight of heavy silk brushing against my cheek. I had become a different person. Dark brown or black would have been more me, but let it go for now. Perfection cannot be attained in the first attempt.

My cousin had a full-sized mirror inside her wardrobe in which I now recognised me as I had never recognised myself in

a mirror before. It took me a long time to decide between the bur-
gundy red and the star-blue dress. In the end I decided that the
blue one would go better with my blonde wig. Hastily I put it on.
It fitted, a bit tight, but my cousin must be exactly my height and
just that bit slimmer than I. It was very good: not the kind of perfection which I would achieve later in my life, when I knew how
to show off my best side, hold my breath for a firmer posture, to
pull back my arms, because I looked better that way – but then I
could not see the imperfections yet. To me at that moment what
I was seeing in the mirror was the perfect I.

Over the next few days I worked hard at perfecting that image:
I carefully shaved before retiring to my room, creating that peach-
like surface on the skin of the face which was necessary to go with
the blonde hair, removing all hair in my armpits and shaving my
legs to a smoothness that convinced even me. Sitting in front of
the mirror I exercised putting my legs neatly alongside each other,
one knee touching the other, and moving my hands in the manner
other females had been able to acquire nearly unconsciously over
many years of apprenticeship from their mothers, their peers,
from photographs in women's magazines, from film stars. It was
a harsh school I had to go through, because the parts of my body
again and again went out of my control, my knees spread apart, I
got cramps in my legs, my arms lost the grace of movement.
Every movement perfected was an intense joy celebrating my
control over my body. This art, perfected in the loneliness of my
cousin's bedroom, to me seemed like the making of fireworks, the
perfectly purposeless consumption of explosive energy, neither
driving a machine nor intimidating an enemy by destruction, and
therefore the only truly great art.

Let me here dispel some misconceptions which I have heard
often from men obviously uncertain about their gender identity
and therefore aggressive and decidedly stupid when they discuss
what they call transvestites. I am not a homosexual, although as
a woman I want the work of art which I create with so much care

to be attractive to men. But I have no desire to have sex with anybody, man or woman, if anything I imagine myself in embrace with myself, I picture myself to be the woman who is embraced by myself, man and woman at the same time, or something which is neither man nor woman nor beyond that distinction. Perhaps what I want to achieve can best be compared with that Greek painter who painted a bunch of grapes so lifelike that the birds came to peck at them: deceiving their eyes and their desire. My most intense enjoyments are characterised by this lack of purpose, even by what most people would call sterility, a lack of offspring, this sheer aestheticism of the creator of a perfect image.

There was one thing missing at first: I could not expose this wonderful work of art to the eyes of anybody except myself in the mirror. It was unthinkable and impossible to smuggle this woman in and out of the room of my cousin, because as far as my aunt was concerned that room was temporarily inhabited by a male person, and a woman slipping in and out of that room would have insulted her proprieties. I was thus left, every night, to my entirely narcissistic pleasures, yet yearning for an audience, a spectator, a male lured by this wonder of skin, hair and dress, the laughter of eroticism, and the brilliance in my blue eyes. But at that stage of my art it was perhaps a bit too early to expose this artifice to the eyes of spectators and critics. So it was all for the good that I gave myself a whole summer of the most intense training in womanhood in the seclusion of that feminine room.

In this way the vacation passed quickly, until one evening while I was fully dressed up, the door which I had negligently forgotten to lock was opened and a young man entered without knocking.

For a moment he stared at me, and stammered: But, but, where is Frank? Are you a friend of Frank?

How dare you enter this room without knocking, I screamed with the best imitation of female fury surprised in the act of self-admiration I could then present.

Well, it is my room, after all. For a moment I forgot that Frank was still here.

Don't lie to me, I said disdainfully. This is the room of Frank's cousin.

Well, I am Frank's cousin.

But Frank's cousin is a girl, I said uncertainly.

Suddenly he laughed: And Frank is a boy!

He closed the door and took off his jacket.

This is funny, he said. Now everything but that! My cousin dresses up as a girl. Wonderful!

I blushed deeply. How had he found out? What did I do wrong?

As if he had read my mind, he said: Oh, you are perfect, darling, absolutely perfect. No need to worry, there is nothing wrong with your disguise, and anywhere but in my room you would have fooled me, you are just in the wrong place. You see, I know my aunt, and I know that you would never dare to bring a girl to your room in my aunt's house. So it can only be you, Frank. And the other thing is, of course, that since I dress up as a man, my mind is open, I at least consider the possibility that the appearance may just be hiding something else. Besides, you are wearing my dress.

Of course, it's her clothes, her wig, her stockings. Of course! How could I have forgotten this?

So, you are Jane, I said softly.

OK, she said, take off that dress.

But I can't, I said, not with you here. What would your aunt say?

Ah stop it, don't play the coy little girl with me, not with me. My aunt is sound asleep, or else I would not have come in dressed like this. At this time of the night there is nearly nothing that will wake her.

But you are . . . a girl.

And you are . . . a what? she laughed. Caught you nicely, didn't

I? Right! Let's have a nice, slow strip! I enjoy a good striptease.

She flopped down on the chair and watched me as I slowly took off the blue party dress. When she saw my bra, she laughed. I took off my nylon stockings, my bra, and then hesitated.

Come on, don't torture me, she shouted. Get on with it. My, you are beautiful. I never thought that men could be beautiful like that. Nothing to be ashamed of. So, come on, take it off. Reveal everything!

I had an idea: Only if you strip for me as well!

Oh, come off it, girl! Since when do men strip for women?

We laughed, but she got up and undressed as well.

In the end we locked the door and went to bed. There was no romance. We had sex, eventually, but having sex is not what it was and is all about. We had sex in the same way in which we showered or had a bath. It was good for our health. The excitement for both of us is somewhere else. She did not look deep into my eyes, and I did not feel my heart flutter or a sob rising in my throat, there were none of the sentimental clichés of teenage romance. But there and then we decided we were perfect partners for each other. We were good for each other.

Five years later, my cousin and I married. Jane completed her accountancy course and was offered a post in a large chain of supermarkets, eventually becoming manager of the local branch. I completed my course in law, took a post in the civil service, and made my way up to section head. We are very well off, although the tax is quite heavy for two people who earn so well, but then with our combined expertise we have found many ways to reduce that burden. We don't have any children. We are a perfectly normal couple.

I admit that in the beginning it was extremely strenuous to keep my male and my female body apart. I had to concentrate on being a man all the time when I was in the office. I was constantly aware that I was deceiving people when I walked around in men's clothes, but also when I walked around in women's dresses. I had to be constantly alert to the fact that I was some-one other than the person I would have others believe me to be. I dreaded the possibility of being found out. For a long time I lived a daily crisis, the expectancy of a catastrophe. Later it became like being bilingual: I switched easily and perfectly from the body language of the man to that of the woman.

Having Jane as a friendly critic and a mine of insider informa-tion was of course useful, although she always showed a certain disdain for the sartorial and psychological problems of women. But she remembered and noticed little gestures like the move-ment with which women after a wild dance or after playing ten-nis wipe loose hair out of their faces, she would laughingly remember the admonitions of her teenage years and throw them at me whenever she found fault in my posture or grooming: Don't stick your tummy out! Pull your tummy in! Stand up straight! You look like a witch! You need to wash your hair. You can't wear your hair like that, you look like a whore! You are eat-ing too much, your midriff is like a car tyre! No waistline at all!

While she herself found this whole feminine masquerade, as she called it, ridiculous and imprisoning, she had as a girl gone through the entire learning process that tells us which colours will achieve particular effects – take black, my dear, it makes you look a bit thinner – which pattern, which textile structure was needed to conceal one of my many bodily defects. Things like this are difficult to learn when you are no longer a child, just as it is nearly impossible for an adult to acquire a new language with the same kind of perfection with which a child learns it. But I made progress, I learned the entire repertoire of camouflage, concealment, intonation, and flattery necessary to present my-self as a woman in public, and soon, after poring over all the women's magazines from overseas, I learned the most sophisti-cated tricks to suggest that my body was like those of the man-nequins in fashion plates. I even began to correct Jane, who no longer troubled herself to keep up with the knowledge necessary to present a perfect feminine appearance. Very soon I was buying her clothes to wear to the office, and she complimented me on my exquisite taste.

At first we kept our passion for dressing up strictly within the home and to the hours when our servants left the house after dinner or on their free weekends, but once a year we went on an extended holiday overseas. We did not choose the beaches where one walks around in bikinis and bathing trunks, because bikinis and bathing trunks are a bit too treacherous for our kind of game. For us to create the effect we want to create we need something more elaborate than these tiny bits of cloth. So we usually chose the winter in Europe or America, and one of the larger cities.

While Jane had worn her suit in public, away from the house of my aunt, right from the beginning – it is much easier for women to wear men's suits than it is for men to wear women's dresses – I found it hard to adjust to the idea of walking out of my hotel suite in women's clothes. I was watching myself nervously, trying not to fall into the most common mistake of men imitating women, mincing along like a sparrow, swinging my hips in an exaggerated fashion, trying desperately to be natural and relaxed. It took me some time before I learned to move in the world, self-assured and secure, accepted in refined and distinguished company. For me that dress, at least in the beginning, was not meant to take anyone in, it was a very private game in the seclusion of my bedroom, but when we eventually ventured forth for the first time from our room in a good hotel in Berlin it did take them in, all of them, it was really good theatre, the best, I would say, without being arrogant: it worked, every time.

In fact, once it worked catastrophically well. That was in New York. Jane had gone ahead down to the bar, where she would engage in friendly backslapping and equally friendly exchanges of anecdotes and more or less stupid or risky jokes, the kind of stories men tell each other over a glass of beer or whisky, while I worked carefully on my dress and my appearance to create a stunning impression when I entered the dining-room later that night. So when I finally walked along the hotel corridor alone, I suddenly found myself facing this young man, hardly twenty, who looked at me with that burning in his eyes which I had come to recognise, but of such intensity that I grew frightened. Women are of course not only objects of male desire, they themselves have a hand in creating themselves as such objects, but many men in their boundless stupidity and with their one-track minds constantly misread the signals which a woman sends out by the way she moves, dresses and behaves. The signal is clearly not "Drag me off to bed and rape me!" but "Admire me in all my female glory! Desire me and love me!" But most men have a surprisingly limited repertoire of reactions to beauty. The only thinking parts of them are their hormones and their reproductive juices. They are characterised by a complete lack of aesthetic intelligence. This, I immediately understood, was such a one-track mind.

On the other hand, I suddenly realised, this wonderful work of art I had created had finally produced the reaction which I had not intended, but which I should have been able to predict: the work of art had advertised a commodity which did not exist. But now suddenly there was a buyer who wanted the goods. He didn't and couldn't understand that this advertisement was its own completely useless wish-fulfilment. That there was no depth behind the shiny surface which could be bought or stolen.

I tried to brush past him nonchalantly, but he stopped me.

Please, he said in a voice quivering with intensity, slight patches of red chasing over his cheeks and his forehead, come with me, and he opened a door.

Young man, I started, with my most forbidding face. What do you think you are doing?

Come, he repeated, but he had already grabbed my wrist and threw me through the open door into his room, slammed the door, locked it, and looked at me, half-shivering, half-enraged. He took off his jacket, looking at me all the time with that salivating idiocy which is so characteristic of male sexuality, opened his fly, nestled inside, and then turned to me. At that moment I tried to storm past him towards the door, but he caught me.

There was a short struggle, while he tried to pin me down on the bed and tear away my panties, I tried to kick him with my knee in his groin, but failed, he shouted at me, I am going to kill you, if you try that again! and then suddenly he stopped, laughed, shouted, ranted, cried, shrieked:

You swine! You fucken homo bastard! You bloody cheat! You bloody mother-fucker! You cock-sucker! You arse-fucker!

With that he started to tear at my dress, which came off my body in shreds, this wonderwork of silver and pink from an exclusive boutique in the Village, he tore the wig from my head, laughing maniacally, shrieking, he tore off my bra, he started to beat me, raining blows on me, he kicked me, his fists hammered on my belly, while all the time his half-erect cock danced a ridiculous dance out of his fly, finally he pushed my face into the bed, and then, shrieking, began to rape me.

Terrified, my body in pain as if somebody had trampled all over me, feeling dirty, I lay on the bed, while he buttoned up his fly, not looking at me any more, his face now ashen white, as if surprised at an act he had not thought himself capable of before, and, putting on his jacket with trembling hands, walked out of the room. I lay there for a long time, not knowing what to do. My dress was in shreds, my mind was swirling, I could not think, except: there is nothing I can wear, I cannot walk back to my room in the nude. I cannot walk back to my room so humiliated. Whose room is this anyway? What if the owner of the room comes back and finds me like this? I started to cry, my body racked by spasms, howling, water and snot streaming down my face, helpless, lost.

It took a long time before I was able to think again. I finally got up, opened the cupboard, rummaged around until I found a pair of pyjamas which fitted me and a man's dressing gown. With that I made my hurried transit to my room, clutching the shredded remains of my clothing. What hurt was not only the fact that I had been used, that I had been humiliated, violated, that my body had been beaten and served as a mere hole in which this idiot could rub his penis. What hurt me was that this maniac had destroyed the artifice of my femininity, had debased the work of art to a mere plastic wrapper around my body, to be torn to shreds so as to consume me.

I phoned Jane in the bar, and told her: I have just been raped. Jane laughed and laughed: I don't believe it! I don't believe it! But eventually she came up to our room.

I told her that I had lost the confidence to go out for dinner. I just wanted to rest. Jane ordered a dinner in our room.

We talked about this until late that night. Jane was very understanding and made me feel a bit better, but we both understood that there was nothing we could do to this bastard, even if we caught him. Any attempt to get him for rape would end in ridicule and embarrassment, not to talk about the chance that news of this incident would finally reach my department in the civil service. We decided to cut short our visit to New York and fly back to South Africa the next day.

The story has a sequel. Two years later, in Paris, I met my rapist again. Jane and I were in a little bar. He was sitting two tables away from us. I pointed him out to Jane. In an instant Jane was up, an imposing sight, her broad, square shoulders emphasised by the jacket she was wearing, the man saw him coming, then saw me, there was a sudden fright in his eyes, he jumped up, ran towards the entrance, Jane followed him. I got up too and walked towards the entrance. There, on the sidewalk, Jane turned into a savage fighter, hit, kicked and hammered him. She had taken karate at the age of fourteen, and had been very good at it. Hard as nails.

The guy was down, bleeding, stammering: Stop it! Stop it!

What did I do to you? Then there was the whistle, and the cops arrived. The barman must have alerted them.

Jane, all affronted, shouted: You touch my wife again and I'll kill you! and hit him again. For show as much as to really hurt him more.

The French understand jealousy. But they had to take us to the police station. One of the flics threw me an admiring sideways glance. He understood how two men could get into a fight over me. Quite natural, really, isn't it?

In her deposition, Jane gave my name, I gave hers, and the little coward did not dare to reveal his and my secret, and demurely gave what I believe was his real name. Jane made up a story in which she accused the man of touching me in an insulting and lewd manner, he protested mildly, but in the end, we all had to pay a fine for disturbing the peace, we were warned to behave and let go.

As we left the police station I said to Jane: Typical male macho aggression! Do you always have to make such a spectacle of yourself?

We both laughed until we cried tears.

Finally he said: What did you expect? That I take the rape of my wife lying down?

No, I said, nobody can expect that. That would be unnatural.

A naartjie in our sosatie

WHEN THE SLOGAN *A naartjie in our sosatie* appeared on the walls of Cape Town, together with the capital A's in the circle, Jean-Jacques Marais had already been dead for a few years, so there is no obvious connection between him and the slogans. Besides, very few politically active people still knew Jean-Jacques, and the few who knew him apart from me on the whole did not like him at all. As far as I know, very few people were influenced by him in the years before his death when he was on pension and lived in Zululand, because that was a time when Althusser and Polantzas were the fashionable political thinkers. I, at least at that time, had never come across anyone who had read Kropotkin or Bakunin except Jean-Jacques and his young wife Anna, about twenty years his junior. There were some rumours that he had been relegated from his post as master at a well-known school in Dijon because he had an affair with one of his female (others said: one of his male) students; and Anna had been a student in his Russian classes at the University of Grenoble, where he had found a post as a senior tutor after his relegation from the school, just before they married and had to leave France.

Jean-Jacques and Anna had fled from France in 1940, as she

was the daughter of a well-known German-Jewish writer, and they had survived in South Africa because Jean-Jacques soon became well known as a child photographer among the rich Jews of Johannesburg. She found a job as a secretary in a large stock-brokers' firm, and when they had established themselves after the war, Jean-Jacques, who had a Doctorate d'État in German and Russian, looked for a post in a university or college. To make contact with the university and to refresh his grasp of the subject, he did an MA at the University of Cape Town on Thomas Mann's *Felix Krull*.

There were, of course, soon rumours that Jean-Jacques was an ardent disciple of Bakunin and an anarchist, and several profes-sors on the selection committee for the post of senior lecturer in the German Department were adamantly against his appointment, even dragging up the entirely unproven and possibly unfounded rumour about him having seduced (by now) several of his pupils while a schoolmaster, and some of his students, including his later wife. A libertine and an anarchist, what next! they asked their col-leagues, not in committee, because the University of Cape Town is a liberal institution, but over tea. Nevertheless, his impressive French doctorate and his MA with distinction, his excellent ref-erees' reports and the very positive votum of the head of the department secured him the post, and from then on he taught Old High German and Middle High German in the department.

When talking about Jean-Jacques I mustn't forget Edgard, of course, an undergraduate student who majored in German and Philosophy at that time, but then Edgard was an anarchist of another sort, and had little patience with Kropotkin or Bakunin, although he had a kind of grudging respect for Jean-Jacques.

How can you trust an anarchist, Edgard would argue against Bakunin, who while he says that freedom can never proceed from authority wants to put children into school? A man who wants to eliminate God from school because he is the eternal slavemaster, but not the teacher who has become his secular representative on earth? Who argues that the principle of authority is legitimate and natural in the education of children? Who believes that out of this authoritarian education can eventually emerge free people? Come off it, that is not anarchism! By sending children to school you produce docile little people who will never know what to do with the freedom you will generously give them.

Edgard had as a student already published two slim volumes of poetry which had disappeared without a ripple in the generally uncivilised atmosphere of Cape Town, but had elicited two rather positive reviews in London and New York, and had earned him a minor poetry prize for a first volume. After that he stopped writing and took to drinking. Reality, he maintained, does not conform to our way of thinking, and the poetic metaphor is only the most outrageous way of creating the fiction of coherence in an incoherent universe. There is no order or governance in reality, reality is *an-arche*, chaos. In order to adjust our minds to the real reality which is usually hidden because it disappears behind our ordering intellect and behind language, we have to block our outer grey cells with some kind of intoxicant.

Anarchism for Jean-Jacques on the other hand was less an immediate experience, more something which became a reality for him as a theoretical concept and as a history he had read about. As a student Jean-Jacques had used his school holidays for pilgrimages to the sacred places of anarchism. So he had gone to Bern's Bremgarten cemetery where Bakunin is buried and was most distressed that the Swiss did not seem to have appropriated the very simple message of anarchism, which in his view would fit in so well with some of the basic tenets and traditions of Swiss democracy: Anarchism, he instructed his newly-found Swiss friends in a pub, attempted to achieve a human order without authority and without government, in solidarity and in the form of cooperatives, not all that different from the way the Ur-Kantone worked. But despite all the lip-service which the Swiss paid to the spirit of William Tell in speeches made on national holidays, there was little if any enthusiasm for bringing these ideals back to life in the twentieth century. Yet, even though the local population was totally uninterested in the ideas of his hero, Bern remained for Jean-Jacques the centre of world anarchism, and the place where the first anarchist newspaper, the *Arbeiterzeitung*, had appeared. He spent his time during that vacation in the reading hall of the Swiss Landesbibliothek reading up on the history of Swiss anarchism. On his way home he traversed the Swiss Jura and looked for the remnants of the Swiss anarchist movement, but was nearly beaten up by some Jura farmers in a pub when he exclaimed: "Vive le Jura libértaire!" With the immortal words "Damned son of a pig!" they threw him out on to the road. During the next vacation he was arrested in Franco's Spain, and spent a few weeks in a Spanish jail, because he was asking too many questions about the Catalonian anarchism.

In Cape Town in the late fifties Jean-Jacques had organised an anarchist study circle, which was not only attended by two philosophy students and Edgard, but had attracted a "coloured" Trotskyist, interested in the early history of socialism, and four black men whom Jean-Jacques had helped to learn to read, write and do some basic arithmetic at the evening school for black workers, while instilling in them the principles of Kropotkin and Bakunin, whenever the "principal" of that school, a strictly Marxist trade unionist, was not looking. This evening school was at that time arranged by lecturers and students of the University of Cape Town as a kind of social penance for being white. It was here that Jean-Jacques tried to create an anarchist movement in South Africa, spending a lot of time on the attempt to transmit the ideas of Bakunin to his audience.

He would expound the basic ideas of anarchism: We reject all privileged, official and legal law-making, authority and manipulation, even if it arises out of a system of one person one vote, because we believe all this hocus-pocus only serves to distract us from the fact that all laws made by the state are made in favour of a privileged minority against the interests of the oppressed majority.

One of the four black workers in our circle, Willy Nzimande, later joined the ANC and became a key figure in Umkhonto we Sizwe, but he carried on writing to Jean-Jacques until the latter died; a second, Jack Ntunzi, was persuaded to join the Unity Movement, became one of the most knowledgeable proponents of Trotsky, and lost no opportunity to fiercely attack anarchism as a form of bourgeois egoism; the other two, Marshall Ngwenya and Terror Mzimane, who had by then become members of a radical-left splinter group of Poqo, were caught attempting to blow up the appellate court in Bloemfontein, and, sentenced to life imprisonment, both died on Robben Island about three years ago.

Marx's main fault, Jean-Jacques said, was that he was dogmatic like all professional academics and researchers. He believed in his theories in an absolute way and from the height of this theory he despised everyone else as mere amateurs.

Hold on! Hold on! interjected Manie, the coloured Trotskyist, Marx was the father of scientific socialism, and science is the very opposite of dogmatism.

Marx considered himself the Pope of Socialism, Jean-Jacques replied, in which belief he was bolstered by his sycophants and blindly supportive friends who only thought through him and in his words. He used the word "science", but he behaved like the most skilled Jesuit dogmatist when it came to critics and opponents. He was an authoritarian communist who wanted to bring about the freedom of the workers through the centralised power of the state.

Having just discovered the heady raptures of arguing within a highly structured socialist theory, I violently objected to this view of Marx and his work, but Jean-Jacques smilingly fielded all my objections with a kind of good-natured, apparently relaxed and unstructured banter, which, however, always proved to be highly informed and intelligent in retrospect.

143

The state, Edgard mumbled in his slightly drunken state, is a mere chimera, one of our totally inept attempts to impose order on a disorderly universe, and because of that ineptness the attempt has totally failed, creating its own disorder out of the stupefying desire for law and order. The four black workers laughed, although their English was not yet quite up to the more intricate logic of this statement. They really got a first-rate education in debate in this circle.

Really, do we have to listen to the subhuman ruminations of this drug addict? said Manie. I did not come here to listen to this kind of alcohol-inspired bar philosophy. This is nothing but fascist nonsense! The four black workers laughed again, fascinated by this complex way of saying: Throw out the drunken swine.

But, said Edgard, I really believe in holy chaos, the origin of all creativity. Why do we so desire slavery when we all could be Gods? Oh, you are all lifeless corpses!

He had told me once that when he was asked to fill in a form for a passport which contained a question about his religious affiliation, he had written "Chaotist". And long before hippies made wild, uncombed hairstyles fashionable, he walked around with long unwashed hair to demonstrate his opposition to the state, the system and a religion of clean-cut and clean-shaven hypocrites. Some of the professors and lecturers were so incensed by this hairstyle that they threw him out of their classes, but, as he said, you cannot learn anything from a person who is so narrow-minded that he objects to an unusual hairstyle.

The circle, in short, produced the kind of discussion which, with a slightly different vocabulary, took place at that time in small clandestine academic Marxist, ANC, PAC, and Trotskyite circles all over the country, and there would have been nothing memorable about it were it not for the personalities of Jean-Jacques and Edgard. For me they perfectly represented the two possible faces of anarchism.

Edgard conformed more to the popular image of anarchism:

aggressive, unrestrained, deliberately flouting all rules of social intercourse and all laws of society, and often forced to pay heavily because of that. His motto was the motto of the novel *Hyperion* by his most beloved poet, Hölderlin: *Non coerceri maximo, contineri minimo, divinum est*, although it must be admitted that he was always more interested in the first part of that sentence than in the second. He completely rejected anybody who wanted to make his wisdom the law of the world.

Edgard at that time had a girlfriend by the name of Irmi, who walked around in old jeans urgently in need of several patches, her black hair short around her round face, and who accompanied him, smoking endless cigarettes and asking awkward questions about the social commitment of the members of the anarchist circle. She, apparently, worked in an advice office for the unemployed and regarded the circle as a form of intellectual masturbation, but added that she had no objection fundamentally to masturbation, as it produced very interesting forms of pleasure. Irmi, who had been incessantly active in all kinds of ventures from cultural events to political initiatives, seemed to take from Edgard by a kind of silent osmosis this love of fate, the acceptance of any turn in her life, which he had once expressed in the sentence: There is a God in us and he directs our fate like streams of water. They seemed to live in complete harmony, neither seemed to demand from the other what he could not give, and yet they were constantly giving themselves to the other without restraint. It was as if there was a paradise island in the turning whirlpool of Edgard's chaotic mind and the social chaos we were living through then.

Sometimes, when suitably intoxicated, she would proudly pull down her trousers and show off the blue weals which she said were the signs of Edgard's love on her body. Edgard smiled and said: She likes to be beaten and humiliated in bed. This further confirmed Manie's suspicion that in the end Edgard was a fascist, although the picture of the sadist somehow did not fit Edgard's personality. But Irmi remained faithful to Edgard until she was picked up by the police for the distribution of some anti-apartheid pamphlets and sent to jail for four years. By the time she came out of jail Edgard had already left for Germany.

When Manie jokingly said, You must have enjoyed the beatings in jail, you with your masochistic tendencies, she looked at him as if he were out of his mind and said: Are you crazy? Do you think these fascists know anything about sex or erotic lust? They beat you in the same stupid and mechanical way in which they fuck their unfortunate wives and girlfriends. How can you compare Edgard's eroticism with the mindless and vulgar beatings by these thugs?

Towards the end of that year Edgard went on a scholarship to Tübingen to study under the well-known German scholar Beißner, who was the world authority on Edgard's beloved Hölderlin. Despite the fact that he had always denounced me as a power-hungry bourgeois communist swine, he wrote to me regularly, complaining about the philistine nature of the Germans, saying that he now completely understood the despairing letter in Hölderlin's *Hyperion*: Barbarians from time immemorial, who have become even more barbarian by diligence and science and even religion, totally incapable of any godlike feeling, decadent to the bone when it comes to the happiness of grace. I can think of no people who are more destroyed than the Germans. Everything they do and think is mindless and devoid of a soul. Just as Jean-Jacques had not found the spirit of Bakunin in Bern, so Edgard had not found the spirit of Hölderlin in Tübingen.

No more great and noble deeds are possible in this world, he wrote once, because noble deeds today are lost within the welter of degrading and useless information spewed out by publishers, newspapers, radio and television. A world where the colour of the dress of the English queen, the throwing of a little ball on a field of green grass or the inane lyrics of a pop group are of more value than the heroic deed of somebody who saves a life or the immortal poem of a great poet deserves neither the hero nor the poet. Great deeds and great works of art, if they are not received by a noble people, are nothing but a resounding knock on a forehead which no longer contains a brain, poetry today is a beautifully coloured leaf fallen into the indecent garbage of worldwide consumerism. A world in which greatness of deed or mind is not echoed by greatness of deed and mind is a place for passive corpses, not the place for somebody who is still human and alive.

His letters contained fragments of poems he was writing again then, poems I could not make head or tail of, partly because of their fragmentary nature, of course, but mainly because of the very private meanings which they unfolded and the associative jumps which I was unable to follow. One was the beginning of a long poem (he wrote) called *Sons of God*:

Like princes Hercules. Common-sense Bacchus. Christ,
    however, is
The end. He is of another nature, surely, but he fulfils
What presence was missing
Of heavenlies in the others.

A later fragment from that same poem was equally puzzling:

If therefore higher into the heavenly goes
Triumphal march, it will be named, like the sun
By the strong ones, the jubilant son of the highest.
Then there is, like now, the time of poetry.

As far as I could ascertain later, the manuscript of this and other poems must be considered lost. He seems to have destroyed all his unpublished manuscripts in Stikland in a burst of self-destruction which ended with an attempted suicide, his last rebellion against the world into which he did not seem to fit.

When he phoned from Frankfurt to say that he was on his way home to Cape Town, I promised to fetch him from the airport and invited him to stay with me for some time. I met him at the airport and was terrified by the impression of bodily and psychic destruction he made on me. This impression was intensified when suddenly, and apparently without recognising me, he started to scream that I, and I alone, was responsible for the loss of his baggage and his mind on the journey from Frankfurt to Johannesburg. You, he screamed, have always been one of those who wanted to make the state a school of morals, Marxist morals in your case, and you never understood that that was the hell of our existence: morals. Prescriptions! You and the other know-betters and dogmatists. The very attempt to make society a sort of heaven makes it the gloomiest sort of hell. You just want to rule with the rulers of the world, you howl with the wolves, you take part in oppressing the people. Everybody turned around to look at us, when he suddenly lurched forward, screamed: Socialist fascist! and hit me so hard with his fist against the head that I lost consciousness.

I awoke several hours later in hospital, and when I enquired after my friend, I was told that he had been charged with public violence and was being held at a police station. I phoned the police officer in charge and said that I would prefer not to press charges against Edgard. But the police had already transferred him to Stikland, where he was undergoing psychological tests. A few days later I heard that he had been diagnosed as paraphrenic and had been committed to Stikland as a dangerous psychopath.

Edgard spent most of the rest of his life in Stikland, and sunk into a kind of stupor, which can be ascribed at least partially to the constant medication but could also be seen as the final defeat of a sensitive, intensely freedom-loving, creative person. Amongst the people who tried to secure his release, besides me, were Jean-Jacques and Anna, who even offered to look after him. But psychiatric officialdom declined this offer with the excuse that Edgard was too dangerous and aggressive to be let loose on humanity.

In the beginning I visited him as frequently as I could, but often spent a totally exasperating hour in his room or on a bench in the garden with him. He would either not talk at all or babble incoherent, banal nonsense. But one afternoon while we were lying in the shade under a tree, and after he had been silent for half an hour, he suddenly said: There is a forgetting of all being, a silencing of our existence, it is as if I have found everything I was looking for, or – and it seems to be the same to me – I have lost everything I ever had. It is a kind of night without sun or stars or moon. But he did not sound desperate, rather as if he had found a final wisdom and final peace.

At the age of sixty-five Jean-Jacques took his pension and moved with Anna, who gave up a very promising academic career, to the north of Zululand, where he helped an international relief organisation to set up a sugar-producing cooperative among the poverty-stricken blacks of the region. He succeeded at least in reducing some of the worst poverty of the members of that collective, but had endless hassles with the authorities and the other sugar-producers and the sugar-mills, who did not want their monopoly broken by the "natives", and with the members of the cooperative, who never quite approximated his ideal of the human ability to live in an anarchic society. So it came as no surprise when a few years later I heard that he had been killed. While the official story was that he had been killed accidentally in a "faction fight", one of the members of the collective I met later told me that that "faction fight" had been organised by the local farmers and Inkatha, who liked the "anarchism" of Jean-Jacques as little as the "communism" of the ANC.

Just after the death of Jean-Jacques, Irmi and I arranged a reading of Edgard's early poetry, with the idea of reviving the battle for his freedom and raising funds for the court case we were contemplating. About seventy people squeezed into the small hall and sat through the reading on uncomfortable chairs and, I must say, contributed generously to our fund. As I was reading his beautiful poem *The chained stream*, I saw him slide in through the back door and, leaning against the wall, listen to his own poetry. Afterwards we found out that he had been dismissed –

possibly because of the publicity which we had given his case in the weeks before the poetry reading and because of the threat of legal action.

So after the reading we handed him the money we had raised, and he invited us to the pub around the corner. I noticed immediately that Irmi did not know how to react to his freeing: while she had been most vociferous in the struggle for his release, she seemed unable to take up their relationship where it had been interrupted many years ago. So the talk was uncertain and without direction for about two beers, Edgard contributing little, and Irmi being completely silent.

While he was ordering his third beer, Edgard very quietly turned to her and said: These are all swindlers.

Irmi, at a loss what to say, appealed to me with her eyes to say something.

What do you mean? I asked him.

I am not talking to you, he said. You are a swindler, too. Else why are you not in jail or in an institution? An anarchist who is allowed to walk around freely, what a joke!

With that he picked up his glass, threw it to the ground, put all the money we had given him on the bar, and walked out. There was an uneasy silence. Nobody followed him. He came back to the door for one moment and shouted: Except perhaps Jean-Jacques. Then he finally departed.

After that evening I saw him several times among the hoboes in Greenmarket Square and on the Grand Parade, but he completely ignored me, even when I greeted him. After that I finally lost track of him.

But that was the time when the slogan *A naartjie in our sosatie* appeared on the walls of Cape Town.

Children play butcher

IN THE YEAR 1927, WHEN the Mpondos were killing most of their pigs because they believed that the Americans would come in many aircraft and send down lightning and thunder on all whites until they were burned to death and because they were told that the fat of the pigs would attract the lightning and burn all the inhabitants of the hut where these animals were kept, the two sons and the daughter of a nearby farmer had stolen away from the farm and were watching the spectacle of such a pig slaughter. One after the other the animals were held down by a helper and killed by a quick movement of the big butcher's knife. While they were bleeding to death, one of the men held a bowl under the spurting throat because it was believed that such blood smeared on the body made one immune against the lightning to come. After each killing all the participants in this ritual held up the red side of their ICU cards to heaven, thus inviting the Americans to come now and deliver them from the oppression of the whites and from their poverty.

The spectacle had something of a great festival about it, an occasion on which all these poverty-stricken peasants and workers anticipated their freedom to come, and the death squeals of the pigs, which were slaughtered and immediately cooked and served to all family members, friends and bystanders, mixed with the sounds of drums and shouting and singing. Some saw the slaughtering of the pigs, which were often seen as "white" animals, as anticipating the slaughter of white colonialists that was to follow, and so the men who performed the slaughter went to their task with particular pleasure. Only one member of the kraal spoke very powerfully against the eating of pork, which he said was impure and infected all those who ate the meat with impurity. The other members of the kraal laughed about him good-naturedly, because they had eaten pig meat for some time now, and nothing very drastic had happened to them. They were not going to give up a great feast for the confused ideas of a religious fanatic.

The three children who watched the whole procedure from the nearby bushes, which concealed them from the inhabitants of the kraal, observed with great fascination both the slaughter and the drumming, dancing and singing that accompanied it. Fully involved in their game of spying "on the kaffirs", they completely forgot the time, and when the dusk came suddenly they were still in the bush above the kraal. Hastily they beat their retreat into the darkness which descended quickly. When they came home they were given a thorough beating for staying out late, for going down to the "kaffir kraal" and for not informing their mother where they were. Their mother was crying: she thought that they had been killed, and she made them swear that they would never do this again.

The next morning, while their father was out looking after the cattle and their mother was bathing the baby, the six-year-old Frans said to the five-year-old Hannie: Let us play butcher! and Hannie said: Yes, that is exciting. And they said to the four-year-old Henning: You be the little pig and I will be the butcher, and Hannie is going to assist me. So Frans fetched the big knife from the kitchen and Hannie fetched a bowl and all three of them went behind the house. Frans said: But you must take off all your clothes. Pigs do not wear clothes. No, said Henning, that is not allowed. But then we can't play, said Hannie. You must! So they took little Henning and undressed him, even if he didn't like the game any more.

Right, said Frans, get down on your knees and your hands like a pig. But I don't want to, this is not nice. Please, let me go. And Hannie said: Don't spoil the game, do as Frans tells you. So Henning got down on his knees, and Frans took the knife and stuck it in his brother's neck, exactly as he had seen it at the kraal. And Hannie held the bowl underneath the neck and caught the blood as it spurted out of the neck into the bowl. At that moment Henning started to scream like a pig, and the mother heard his screams in the house, where she was bathing the baby in a zinc bathtub. She let go of the baby, ran to the window, saw the blood and the knife, and stormed out of the house in a rage of red. When she reached the three children, she drew the knife out of the child's neck, and screaming: You murderers, you murderers! hit out with the knife towards Frans, the blade slipped through his ribs and into his heart, and still raging, she hit out towards Hannie and forced the knife into her body as well, and Hannie let fall the bowl with the blood, and fell screaming to the ground, where Frans was lying, no longer screaming but pale in his face.

For a moment the mother looked vacantly at the scene, the three children lying on the ground, the blood everywhere, the bloody knife in her hand, then she dropped the knife, and remembering the baby, she ran into the house. But the baby was no longer breathing, his face turned down under the water, he lay still. The mother snatched the baby from the bath, lifted him up, kissed him wildly, tried to make him breathe again by pressing her lips against his mouth and forcing her breath into his lungs, but the lungs refused to work, and the baby, still warm from the bathwater, was dead. The mother dropped the baby, ran out into the yard again, saw the three children, no longer breathing in the pools of blood, ran into the house, ran out again, took the washing line from between the two trees, got a chair from the kitchen, stood on the chair, fastened the washing line to a branch of the tree and around her neck, and kicked away the chair.

Late in the evening her husband came home, saw the three children in the yard and his wife hanging from the tree, and before he could even enter the house, he collapsed and died with a face which was suddenly red and then paled slowly. The last thing he saw was a silver aircraft murmuring through the sky from the northeast to the southwest.

The greenhouse effect

GRAND DUKE PAWEL IVANOVICH MANILOV, the grand-son of a Russian émigré, whose grandfather and father had made their money first in the rag trade, but soon bought a number of factories and farms, and finally enriched themselves by large-scale speculation on the stock exchange, in the insurance business and in merchant banking, had offered the South African govern-ment a considerable sum of money to sell him Robben Island. There he proposed to build his palace in the middle of an existing nature reserve, which he intended to expand by demolishing all the buildings that might remind him of the time when Robben Island was the university of the revolutionaries. When the South African government refused to sell him Robben Island, and after an equally unsuccessful attempt to buy Seal Island in False Bay, he persuaded the municipalities of Strand and Gordon's Bay to give him permission to construct his own island in False Bay. This permission was granted despite massive protests by the ecology lobby, and Grand Duke Pawel Ivanovich Manilov spared no ex-pense to erect an artificial island and a splendid palace in the wa-ters of False Bay. Thus separated from the herd, as he expressed it, he created his own completely artistic and aesthetic world, which, however, carried in its conception the future catastrophe.

Because one thing is certain, the green lobby was finally vindicated: in whatever small and insignificant way the very building of the island, the burning of petrol and oil used in driving the machines to transport and prepare the material, contributed to the final calamity to which it succumbed.

I was invited to the *soirée* which the Grand Duke gave in his palace on the artificial island to celebrate the discovery of the manuscript of the anonymous late medieval choral work *Herre got, dir sungen schône* by Constantin du Plessis, professor of music at the University of Cape Town and expert in late medieval choral music. I owed my invitation to the fact that the Grand Duke was very interested in a relic of the French Revolution which had been in the possession of my family for nearly two hundred years: the blade used in the guillotine with which Robespierre was beheaded. The Grand Duke had a considerable collection of memorabilia and implements used by revolutionaries to murder legitimate heads of state and other revolutionaries of whom they no longer approved. His greatest treasure was the gun with which Tsar Alexander was shot by the Russian revolutionaries. While I was tempted by his considerable offer, I pretended to be adamant that I would never part with this family heirloom, because I wanted to see if I could not raise the price even further. The invitation was an attempt by the Grand Duke to further these negotiations. In turn, for a young and as yet unknown writer like me, such an invitation had all the possibilities of opening up doors to the inner circles of culture both in this colonial outpost of European culture and, of course, where it really mattered, in Europe. It was my particular bad luck that this very party, to which I was invited, wiped out in one fell swoop the entire cultural elite of South Africa. All the more important therefore is this report by the only survivor of the catastrophe about the proceedings of that most memorable evening, of which the *Times Literary Supplement*, by the way, gives an entirely erroneous impression.

Since the Grand Duke had an allergy against the barbaric sound of motor boats and had successfully lobbied the municipality of Gordon's Bay to ban all motor-driven boats in the vicinity of his artificial island, and had even lobbied Parliament to make this municipal by-law a national law, the only way to reach his island was by a fleet of rowing boats, which ferried guests from Gordon's Bay harbour, a very uncomfortable ride when the incessant Southeaster whipped up the waves in False Bay. But even the great poet Ben Waters, who became seasick even in the calmest waters, climbed into one of the rowing boats manned by half a dozen black servants and stoically braved the harrowing ride to this last outpost of European culture, over the sea, separated from this barbaric slab of a continent by the purifying waters of the ocean, as did the culturati from Bishopscourt and Upper Newlands, shrieking, it is true, whenever a wave threatened to capsize the boat.

When I walked over from the place where I had parked my Volkswagen Golf to the harbour on that fateful evening, I met Waters, whom I knew from a few poetry readings in a very elite circle in Llandudno. He greeted me, and when he heard that I had been invited to the island, expressed his surprise at my selection with a monosyllabic "Oh!" At the harbour we met Professor Paul Kruger van der Merwe (not the well-known Indo-Germanic linguist but the expert on Francesco Manfredini) who had been flown in from Durban by the Grand Duke, and Dr Marianne Haferstroh, the art historian from Pretoria, whose monograph on Karl Friedrich Schinkel had brought her worldwide recognition amongst Schinkel experts. Professor Van der Merwe tried to draw us into a discussion on the authenticity of the find of his colleague from Cape Town (which he very much doubted, and rightly so, as Professor Mandelstrom from the University of Ohio was to prove only two years later). Dr Haferstroh enquired from me whether the boat ride to the island was safe, to which I could only reply: I suppose so, since this was my first invitation to the palace. Waters, who had overheard her question while listening to Van der Merwe, uttered an oath to the effect that the boat ride was pure hell, and the horrible price one had to pay for admission to the most exquisite cultural events in South Africa.

Waters, the only South African poet ever invited to the island, never referred to any South African object in his poetry, be it the astonishing flowers of the veld, the varied and interesting fauna of the Kruger Park, or God forbid, its barbarian inhabitants, both white and black. When he spoke about South Africa at all it was as his Tomi, the place of exile and cultural deprivation, despite the fact that he was born and educated in Cape Town. In this sentiment he agreed with all those who belonged to the *Inner Circle*. His poetry, informed by the austere formal beauty of Petrarchan sonnets and Russian formalist literary theory, used external objects as symbols of exquisite psychological experiences, and showed a studied disdain for anything as vulgar as life or nature. In his one and only critical essay, *The ecstasy of pure being*, he had argued that *any* narrative, because it essentially embraced becoming and thus change, was a compromise with vulgar taste and that Tolstoy's great novels were nothing but the forerunners of such inanities as the American TV serials.

At this moment he was expounding to Van der Merwe the idea that the aesthetic experience had been undervalued ever since that boor of a German philosopher, Hegel, wrote his *Ästhetik*. The barbaric overvaluation of theory and knowledge, he said, was the very evil which was a sign of modernity. He spoke the word "modernity" as if it was an unutterable swear word.

Our conversation was cut short, as soon as the rowing boat left the harbour of Gordon's Bay, by the howling Southeaster, the lurching motion of the boat in the large waves with white horses on them, and the continuous vomiting of the great poet, who attempted but did not always succeed in directing his expectorations over the bow. Van der Merwe, Dr Haferstroh, and I presume myself, were cowering with paper-white faces in the boat which to our untrained eye gave the impression that it would founder in every wave. But the well-trained rowers brought us through the tempest to our destination, where we were greeted by the Grand Duke on the steps of the little harbour directing us across the large piazza surrounded by the palace and its two wings. We had arrived on the charmed island of Prospero.

As we entered through the classical portico into the spacious entrance hall, where we left our nautical outer shells, and then made our way through the throng of guests towards the concert hall, Dr Haferstroh introduced me to Priscilla Clock, the re-nowned critic who wrote for the *Times Literary Supplement*. Ms Clock studied me for a while through her lorgnon as if I was a spe-cially repulsive species of cockroach and then deigned to address me: Ah, I believe you also dabble in the art of writing short sto-ries. And added with a tone which indicated her bottomless con-tempt: South African short stories, I hear, not that I ever read such things. Ms Clock only reviewed Italian, Portuguese and Spanish poetry which had not yet been translated into English: Trans-lations are so awful, so vulgar. A concession to the illiterate, real-ly. Ms Clock also was a member of the *Inner Circle* of the Grand Duke, that is, she belonged to the select group of two dozen cognoscenti who were invited to the intimate evenings of poetry reading and chamber music which he hosted every Wednesday night in the intervals between the four *grandes soirées* of the year, to which he invited the one hundred and twenty people or so in South Africa whom he considered sufficiently well-bred to appre-ciate his exquisite taste and the always extraordinary artistic events he arranged for them. It did not look as if Ms Clock would open up doors to the *Inner Circle* of culture for me.

Drifting away from the stern, disapproving face of Ms Clock, I was hailed by Martin Westermoore, the world-famous sculptor, whom I had met at a rather bohemian drinking party in Obser-vatory, where he had undressed his girlfriend Lucia in a great act of passive striptease. While Westermoore, having no taste for Music or Poetry, did not attend the meetings of the *Inner Circle*, he was invited to the *grandes soirées*, and once a year exhibited his three best sculptures there. The Grand Duke's island was the only place where he deigned to exhibit in South Africa. His regular yearly exhibitions were held in the *Horologe* in Paris, a small but very influential gallery where, besides Westermoore, the three other sculptors of the Non-Realist movement, Fjodor Stepanovitch, Klaus Zur Strassen-Überdom and Italo Calvo, regularly showed their work.

Of course, I would never be so gauche as to mention to him the fact that I had visited the recent Cape Town exhibition *Images of a burning revolution*, but strangely enough, he mentioned this exhibition himself, asking me whether I had seen it. But without waiting for an answer from me, he launched into a long and rather intricate denunciation of struggle art, concluding with the bon mot, which was used by the art critic of the *Weekly Mail* the next Friday (so he must have spoken to Westermoore at the exhibition) as the introductory sentence of his review: It is such a struggle for them to produce art at all that they have to use art as a weapon of struggle to produce art. I did not find the aphorism all that funny, but smiled good-humouredly, because it is very dangerous for any aspiring artist not to find Westermoore witty and *geistreich*.

The concert hall was a medium-sized, intimate space seating about a hundred and fifty people in the style of late eighteenth-century rococo with mirrors on the walls instead of windows. The walls between the mirrors were covered in pictures which would have had pride of place in any European art gallery. While he did not exhibit his one Rembrandt (he would have considered that ostentatious), there were pictures by Lucas Cranach the Elder, Jan Gossaert, Rogier van der Weyden, Albrecht Dürer, Pollaiuolo, Dirk Bouts, Barthol Spranger, and Signorelli. The acoustics were a marvel of sound engineering and the blend of reflecting surfaces and sound-absorbing curtains and chairs gave the hall a delicate reverberation which transformed the most inane music into a magical experience and even coloured any everyday conversation carried on by the people waiting for the concert to begin. As

Westermoore and I entered the concert hall we were met by Professor Pferdemann, a remarkably good-looking man in his late sixties, himself a work of art of Jugendstil qualities, the famous Novalis expert and art lover.

Oh Westermoore, he said, you know that I have just bought that divine little statue of the meditating Zen warrior you had on exhibition in Paris. I was immediately struck by this exquisite tension between the way he carries his armour and his weapons and the complete concentration and submission in the way he meditates. Exquisite.

I had seen the statue in Westermoore's studio before it was sent to Paris. It did not look like a warrior or like anybody in meditation to me at all, and I had secretly dubbed it *Existential non-verbal blob*, although, of course, I would never have been so coarse as to voice such a sacrilege.

What did you think of Singh's performance of Webern's *Passacaglia for orchestra*, the Professor continued. I myself found the first few bars very, how shall I say, fumbling. Like a child searching for the keys. He entered into a long and detailed analysis of the performance, while I slowly moved out of earshot, leaving the unmusical Westermoore to suffer on his own.

It was then that I ran into the Grand Duke himself. The Grand Duke's remarkable massive balding head, what Ms Clock in one of her reviews of the cultural events on the island had called his Russian *Charakterkopf*, rose out of a long, flowing, Russian-style cassock, which emphasised his rotund and massive body, covering everything except his bare feet in leather thongs. He deigned to recognise me, and immediately launched into an attack on the most recent anthology of South African poetry.

You will not believe it, he said. But I am to blame myself. Again and again I tell myself that this land does not produce anything which one should or could call art, sorry, nothing personal implied, of course. But driven by the insatiable thirst of the discoverer of new art I subject myself to the pain of searching for what might be the one unacknowledged talent in South Africa besides Waters.

He paused, looked intensely into my eyes, and said: The pigsty did not reek!

He lifted his hand triumphantly: The pigsty did not reek! You will not believe it, but that is a line from the poems selected to represent the best in South African poetry. I cannot get over it. Not to talk about hippos roaming the ghetto streets. That is the mysticism of an art supposed to lead us to a higher level of insight into the mysteries of existential being: pigsties and hippos! Where, I ask, is that tension of the soul in adversity, which alone trains us in strength? Where in this miserable country is there any depth, any secret, a mask of tragedy, mind or greatness?

Pigsties and hippos! he repeated. He broke into a roaring laughter which filled the hall with delicate reverberating musical echoes: Pigsties and hippos! Everybody turned to look at us and I became aware of the envy in the faces of some who had not been singled out to be addressed by the host personally as I had been.

Pigsties and hippos! he laughed again. No freedom, no delicacy, no courage, no dance, no mastery. It is sad! But every lift which humanity has experienced towards the heights of culture was the work of an aristocratic society, and there is nothing aristocratic about South African society. But I do believe we have to prepare for the performance, you will excuse me. Oh, have you changed your mind about the guillotine blade?

It sounded like an afterthought, but it was the only reason I had been invited at all, and the only reason I had been granted this lengthy interview with the Grand Duke.

I am still thinking about it, I said. I find it hard to part with such an old family heirloom.

He shrugged resignedly, but knowing that in the end he would get what he wanted, and motioned to one of the black servants in eighteenth-century servant's livery, who then began to pass through the crowd of guests, sounding a gong. Within a few minutes everybody was seated on the rococo chairs facing the podium, on which the choir and the soloists gathered, waiting for Professor Constantin du Plessis, expert in late medieval choral music, who was even then led on to the stage by Grand Duke Pawel Ivanovich Manilov, and introduced by him. When the doors were closed it became apparent that the hall was completely soundproof, because even the softest sound of the waves which had reached us before through the open doors was now shut out, and an eerie silence hung over the hall for a second or two, before the Grand Duke began to speak warmly of Professor Constantin du Plessis.

Professor Constantin du Plessis then launched into a long and boring description of how he had found the score of the anonymous late medieval choral work *Herre got, dir sungen schône* in a monastery near Teplice in Czechoslovakia, where it was mouldering in a dusty cellar full of other remnants of the medieval period, which had been dumped there and forgotten by the unartistic fanatics of the Reformation, whom he compared to the barbarian Communists of more recent origin. Of course, all of this was the invention of Professor Constantin du Plessis, who, as Professor Paul Kruger van der Merwe (not the well-known Indo-Germanic linguist but the expert on Francesco Manfredini) had suspected but could not prove, and as Professor Mandelstrom from the University of Ohio was to prove only two years later, had written the manuscript himself, relying on the well-known reluctance of most scholars to crawl through dusty and mouldy cellars of medieval monasteries in Czechoslovakia, in order to add this brilliant discovery to his research record and publication list. (It must be added that Professor Mandelstrom undertook the journey to Teplice merely because his lifelong adversary, Professor Cellini from Amherst College, who had visited Cape Town two months before the performance, and had been present at one of the rehearsals, had written an appreciative review for the *International Review of Music History*, a journal which Professor Mandelstrom considered to be unscholarly trash.) After Professor Constantin du Plessis had ended his introductory remarks, there was polite but enthusiastic applause, and he immediately took the choir into the opening bars of *Genad, heiliger herre mein*. For some time the performance proceeded without indication of the imminent catastrophe, through the aria for soprano, *In dem himmel der engel chron*, and the trio, *Der stern weist uns di recht straß*, to the choral piece, *Des ich der erst moecht gesein*.

The famous tenor Jean-Louis Farçot, who had been flown in specially from Tokyo where he was giving a guest performance, had just launched into the a cappella solo *Magi videntes stellam* when there was a slight tremor which nearly imperceptibly rattled the mirrors on the walls, leaving a faint tinkling sound in the air for several minutes. Some of the guests sat up straight on their rococo chairs with questioning glances, but since the great majority of listeners simply ignored the commotion, and seemed to be totally engrossed in the mellifluous voice of the tenor, they soon settled back and began to listen again to the endlessly winding and monotone *Et stella precedat eos*, sung by the choir and the famous basso Hans Froehlich from the Vienna state opera, who was a house guest of the Grand Duke during the summer months of that year. Without a pause the choir then launched into the slightly frivolous *Caspar, durch dein tugent*.

The choir was just winding its way through the complicated beat of the choral *Für Ihesum den scheppher mein*, which showed a very obvious Arabian influence in the way it treated the drumlike bass line – as my neighbour Mrs Lynette Grace-Jones pointed out to me in a subdued whisper – when a far-off rumbling as if from a thunderstorm added its contradictory beat to the complexity of the chorus. In fact, some of the guests who had not seen the score before the performance for a moment believed that that was part of the choir's attempt to create a specific grandiose effect.

Just as the choir reached the grand finale of the first part, the jubilant *Ir herren, wir schullen froeleich sein*, I noticed the first disjointed little pools of water on the floor. The later explanation of the disaster pointed to a host of contributory factors: the main factor was undoubtedly the inexperience of the builder who was contracted to create the island in False Bay and who had neglected to account adequately for the later consolidation of the rock and sand piled on the sea-floor between the concrete retaining walls and pillars; but there is reason to believe that the sea-floor itself under the enormous weight of the new structure had sagged by about half a metre just before the finale of the first part. Professor Walter Cinders, the renowned oceanographer, pointed out that the main reason for the catastrophe, however, was probably that, coincidentally with these local events, the large ice covering of the Southern Ocean, which had been melting from below for the last fifteen years because of the greenhouse effect, had finally dissolved completely within a week, allowing the glaciers of the interior to slide into the sea and increasing the sea level by one metre and twenty-five centimetres. The effect of this rise of the global sea level reached False Bay and was made more pronounced by the narrowing of the sea in the bay and the gale-force Southeaster at just the moment when the soprano Mariekie van den Heever intoned the brilliant *Venite adoremus Deum quia ipse est Salvator noster* over the subdued humming harmonies of the choir. By this time the isolated pools of water had coalesced and formed one continuous sheet of water, which by now had reached the ankles and was creeping continually up our legs towards our knees. There was some unrest in the hall, but nobody dared to get up.

Even when the hall soundlessly began to tilt towards the stage so that the singers were standing in water which already reached their bellies, while I was still just over knee-deep in water, the choir continued into *Treun ich will folgen dir* and all of the guests remained seated as if glued to their chairs, except for Mrs Lynette

Grace-Jones, who took off her shoes and nylon stockings and wrung out the stockings behind the back of the chair in front of her. It was at this moment, in a short pause before the next aria for Mariekie van den Heever, *Ich sprichs auf die treu mein*, that an ominous gurgling sound was heard in the hall.

I could no longer hold myself down in my seat. As I leapt up, overturning the chair on which I had been sitting, everybody in the hall turned to look at me with a most disapproving scowl on their faces, and their disapproval followed me as I made my way towards the aisle in the middle and up the aisle towards the door. Barbarian! whispered the poet Waters soundlessly but distinctly, as I passed him. Walking over the slimy, tilted floor was extremely difficult, and twice I nearly slipped and fell, but I made my way up towards the door, braving all the stern and disapproving faces. As I turned at the top, the gurgling increased and I saw that the choir was already up to their necks in water, the shorter members had to stretch to hold their heads above the surface, while where I was standing the water already reached my belt.

As I opened the door, a torrent of water rushed into the hall, obliging everybody to get up from their seats. The thunderous roar of the sea suddenly drowned out the singing of Mariekie van den Heever, and despite great efforts on my part, I was unable to close the door again. I hastened towards the portico, but found my progress hindered by both the slipperiness of the floor and the pressure of water. After a few anxious minutes I reached the entrance, opened the door, and was nearly bowled over by a wave which travelled down towards the concert hall unabated. Battling through the waves, I reached the other side of the piazza just in time to jump into the last boat, manned by six sturdy black rowers, leaving the little submerged harbour.

While the men rowed desperately and tried to keep the stern of the boat aligned with the direction of the waves so that we would slowly be pushed towards the shore, they shouted to me to use the tin in the bottom of the boat to bail out the water which constantly rushed over the sides. Sweating and wet through and through, I concentrated on this uncomplicated but tiring task until a sudden lurch and a crunching sound told us that we had run aground. Somewhere ahead of us through the spray of the waves we saw the lights of Somerset West, and as the boat turned over in the surf, I was borne on the crest of a wave towards the sandy shore. All six rowers, none of whom could swim, were washed ashore more dead than alive.

As I gasped on the sand I saw before my inner eye how the throats of the singers on the Grand Duke's island filled with water while they were singing the resounding final *Amen Amen Amen*. By that time it was too late to flee, all the boats had gone, and the palace was sliding into the shallow waters that surrounded it.

Next day I asked a friend, who owned a motor boat and was totally uninterested in the arts, to take me over to the island, but when we reached the place, only one turret still breached the waves. Police boats, marine rescue and many private craft swarmed around the place which had once been the haven of art at the southern tip of Africa. But alas, none of the one hundred and twenty guests escaped the drowning of art on that fateful night. Many divers were busy trying to recover the bodies of the guests and, after I had spoken to the police major, also the irreplaceable treasures of European art, sadly damaged for ever by the waters. The magnitude of the event, almost totally ignored by the South African media, who were concentrating on a slump in the gold price and the current cricket test against New Zealand, was best captured in the next edition of the *Times Literary Supplement*, which carried a three-page memorial article surrounded by black bars mourning the final demise of culture in South Africa.

A ritual in the kloof

A S HE STEPPED FROM THE train at the little station among the vineyards, with the typical insolence of the adolescent, and looked around, he didn't see his father's car. He put the bag over his shoulder and carried the suitcase across the platform and past the little stationmaster's house to the dusty circle in front of the station. Then he waited. The sun burned down from the implacably blue sky, and there was no shade anywhere near. Finally he sat on the stairs of the stationmaster's house.

Thinking vaguely of Cape Town and the boarding school, he stared down the road. As the loneliness of the space invaded him, he felt as if he had sat here many times before, as if sitting and waiting was what his life was about, and as if there would not be anything new ever, and as if he would have to live this over and over again. He was afraid of losing his life in this way, being banished to a dusty little railway station somewhere in the Boland, waiting for old age, suffering, disease and death. He was painfully aware of something else, which for lack of a word he called perfection. He thought of it as being able to do everything he felt himself capable of, thinking interesting ideas, making love, enjoying life, enjoying the power and precision of his body and his mind. Like the sailing boat of his friend's father in False

Bay, bending over in the Southeaster, running into the wind, climbing and rolling over the waves, a perfect machine, and the hands of Max's father on the tiller, the certainty that the boat would not tilt and be buried in the water. But that was not here. Here was only a dusty road, empty.

When the car did not come, he took his suitcase, knocked on the stationmaster's door, and asked whether he could leave the suitcase here for his father to fetch when he came into the dorp. Then he slung his bag over his shoulder again and walked across to the village and along the main road into the open fields and the vineyards towards the farm. There were few people on the road, an occasional car with a cloud of dust trailing after it, a few dark-skinned children walking to town or back to the farm, an old man, a fat woman, her breasts rolling under the bright red dress.

It was a two-hour walk, and he still hoped that his father would come with the car, but the road remained empty and hot. He got thirsty, but there was no water anywhere along the road. All the little streams only ran in winter, when it rained. As he plodded along, the verses he had had to learn off by heart for his last Latin test went through his head and he repeated them as if in a dream:

Ut redit, simulacra sua petit ille puellae
*Incumbensque toro dedit oscula**

The pictures of the nude marble goddess in his Latin book, which he stared at for hours, never came alive to throw their limbs around his aching body. He had to hallucinate a face, a body, an embodiment of his strong feeling when he was in his bed, to caress it, and to be caressed by it, and as he walked he conjured up this body again, made it move, naked, next to him along the road, embracing him from time to time, enticing him to follow her into the vineyards where she promised to do his bidding unseen,

---

* And when he came back, he hurried to the image of his girl, threw himself on his bed and gave her kisses – Ovid on Pygmalion, x, I. 28of.

hidden in the vine leaves, she would crown his head with a wreath of vine, he would be her hero, she would be his, yes, his, entirely, he could take her and do with her as he liked. Finally he gave in to her seductive voice and followed her in among the thick green of the vines, and as she grabbed his life, he suddenly knew all the words which one must speak to a naked woman, a woman who picks you up as you walk along a country road, naked, it was the perfect love, hermaphroditic, she and he were one, locked into each other, and she understood perfectly every movement of his body and moved with him, when he embraced her, he embraced himself, and as he went down on his knees, he experienced this wild love, which took hold of his body and shook it until he reached one glorious explosion, stars shattered his brains, and then after the happiness had been drained from him, and his hand stopped moving, he found himself on the brown earth among the vines, all alone, his trousers hanging above his knees, and his knees dirty from the soil of the vineyard. He knew that he would experience this many more times, this sudden let-down, and that there would be nothing new in it. But he felt too weak to curse this emptiness. He felt crushed and lonely. To think that he would have to do this once more and innumerable times more filled him with despair. If you desire, but do not act, you breed a kind of pestilence. He was groping for an understanding of what was happening to him, but for some time all words escaped him. Then he knew: "exuberance" was the word he was looking for, there was no exuberance. There was too much sameness. There is no reason in what happens, no love in what will happen to you. Sometimes he had felt that thinking was an exquisite delight and he could not understand those of his schoolmates who never seemed to think. They seemed empty and bloated to him. But now he felt that all this thinking was a burden, and he wanted to live in thoughtless ignorance.

He resumed his walk home, dazed, he nearly forgot to pick up his bag, singing a love song he had heard on the radio – *On the island of my desire* – squinting into the burning sun, nearly blinded (he had heard somewhere that masturbation made you blind, but he no longer believed this). As he walked aimlessly, he felt in himself a great freedom. A freedom from any convictions. He felt that he was able to see freely, whereas before he had been blinkered, like his father who had all kinds of principles and convictions. What is the difference between a conviction and a lie? He began to understand that the most common lie is when one lies to oneself. When one does not wish to see what one does see. Belonging to a gang or a group or a church or a party forces one to lie.

When he reached home, his mother stood on the stoep and cried: Franz, I thought you would come tomorrow! Alfred, Alfred, she shouted, look here, Franz is home already. So he had had to walk through the heat and the dust, all this way, simply because of a silly misunderstanding. He hated his mother, her scatterbrained inefficiency. Then he could see she was feeling sorry for him, because he had had to walk all this way, and his eyes followed her as she brought a bottle of Oros and water and poured him a cool drink.

Can I have some ice? he asked. He craved the clean, cold feel of an ice cube on his tongue, but his mother said that ice was dangerous if one was as hot as he was from the walk and that he should first drink the cool drink. She was always full of such stupid precepts, he knew better, because he had ice after cricket, when he was even hotter than now, at the school, and nothing happened to him, just the wonderful feeling of the cold, clear ice on his tongue. Later his father went to fetch the suitcase in the car.

The first few days at home he spent on his bicycle, exploring the neighbourhood, looking for the girls, who, however, were under strict control, and not allowed so much as to speak to him. Only at the farm dam in the valley, when they came to swim in the afternoon in their tightly fitting swimsuits, which emphasised their developing breasts, did he occasionally get near to one, but there were always the others, watching, and there was no way that one could be separated from the crowd. When they had dressed in the bushes and walked away, it seemed to him impossible to ever touch these strange apparitions in their light skirts which sometimes against the sun revealed the shadowy legs, confirming that they, too, were not essentially different from him, that they, too, bifurcated below the tummy, and that they, too, must have something, a dark secret between their legs. But they always escaped him with their giggling voices, and disappeared down the road into the far-off shadows of the trees. So he sat many hours somewhere in the thicket, dreaming of these apparitions and their bodies and of what he would do with them, if only he got one here amongst the bushes. But none ever came to interrupt his dreams.

The time when he had believed that the white sticky substance that flowed from his painfully stiff penis was the sign of some illness, was past. So was the time when he fought his "dirty" thoughts whenever his cock raised its head and forced him into a toilet to make it docile again or the "vile" images which flooded his brain as he dozed off to sleep, with a firm grip on his dick. The tension and the wonderful flightlike release when the white stuff poured out of him had long since got the better of him, and while there was a certain shame attached to these acts, performed in secret places, the lust was more immediate and won out every time against the injunctions of his conscience which had been formed by half-understood biblical stories about Onan and Sodom and Gomorrah, which to him sounded like gonorrhoea. He had for some time now begun to despise the words which were poured into them every morning in chapel, and the word he hated most was "chastity". It was all a lie. He didn't believe that anybody he knew was chaste. Somewhere in the dark, in beds, in sheds, hidden from sight, they all indulged in the pleasure. Sometimes as he dozed off to sleep he felt the world filled with writhing and heaving bodies caught in their tensions and delights, grinning and moaning. Then he cried out and went to the bathroom and took a cold shower. But the images never left him. Not only people, but animals, everything was involved in this strange and exciting dance to reproduce itself. Pain is not the opposite of joy. There is a joy which consists of a rhythm of stimulations of displeasure. He was not certain what happiness meant. He understood that this was nature. Not the beautiful postcards of Cape Point, but the straining and fighting and fucking and multiplying. He had even developed a ritual, where he would kneel in the thickets of the mountainside and dig a hole into the hard earth, symbolising the release he desired but did not dare to contemplate, and then, it was like praying to a long-forgotten female earth deity, water the earth with his seed.

Sometimes, as he walked across the farm, he met the children of the farm workers. They had grown up together, but since he had gone to Cape Town there was a distance between them. They still said hullo, and asked him how it was in Cape Town, and whether he had to learn a lot, but the conversation was monosyllabic. There was one girl, called Hanna, who he had thought to be very beautiful when he was younger, and when he met her he was shy, but she laughed, and said: So, you are having many of these white girls now, you no longer care for your Hanna, do you?

He said, No, that's not true. No, Hanna. No, I am just too busy learning.

Don't lie to me, she answered. I can see, you think of girls all the time.

But he was shy, and did not know what to make of her words, and he was confused that she could see right through to his hidden thoughts, and he blushed. At that she laughed even louder, mockingly, and ran away.

When he was in the bush, he now often dreamed of her without her dress, and he took off her panties and her bra, too. But then she always laughed at him, and he could not do it. Even in the dream. For a few days he slouched around the huts where the farm workers lived, but when he saw her, she was with another of the farm workers' boys, Mark, and she did not even seem to notice him. So he did not go back there. It was useless anyway, he could never marry a coloured. He even heard that if you got caught fucking them, you could go to jail. He deliberately thought this strong word, which he had heard other boys using at school, and believed that he was very brave thinking it. There was a farmer in a nearby valley, he had been taken in by the police one day, and there were rumours among the boys that he had done it with the daughter of one of his workers. But he still regretted that he hadn't tried something with Hanna, when she talked to him. He had a vague idea that that would have been a heroic defiance of an unjust law. In his school they were all against apartheid, it was a church school, but he wasn't sure whether they would have supported him, had he been caught with Hanna. They were anti-apartheid, but they were also anti-sex.

Two weeks into the vacation he met Lourens van Tonder, the son of the café owner in the main street.

You are coming tomorrow? Lourens asked perfunctorily.

To what? he asked.

The testing, Lourens answered.

The testing?

Yeah, the testing, don't you know about it?

No, he said. What testing? What do you test?

Well, if you are a man, or so.

He had heard this often: We will see whether you are a man. And then they had subjected him to all kinds of painful experiences. Rugby, mountain climbing, running a hundred metres. Make you tough. He hated it when others were trying to make a man out of him.

So he asked: And how does that work?

You'll see. Be at the farm dam Sunday afternoon.

When he got there, there were about ten fourteen-year-olds, he knew most of them, he had gone to the village school with them, and saw them on and off since he went to boarding school when he was home for vacations. They stood around in their dirty shirts and shorts, with their knobbly knees, and felt ill at ease. Then came Fisher, and motioned them to follow him into the thicket which covered the kloof above the dam. They walked for about fifteen minutes, in silence. Then they came to a small clearing.

OK, said Fisher, let's see who are the men and who are the boys among you.

They all looked at him expectantly.

Take off your pants, you sissies, he laughed, let's see what you got.

They stood around, not knowing what to do, some blushing, all silent, avoiding each other's eyes.

Well, are you all still pissing and shitting in your pants? Come on, don't be shy. This is where you have to show it.

Eventually, they all took off their shorts and shirts and their underpants and stood around naked, embarrassed. Lanky and gangling, their arms much too long, their knees much too thick for their bodies, they showed the grotesque disproportion of the pubescent. Most of them showed some desultory growth of hair above their penis.

He felt alone, alien, uncomfortable. He was thinking: It is a disease, this bad conscience. But perhaps it is necessary. Perhaps one cannot become aware of the beautiful and the good, if one is not aware of the ugly and the evil. He thought vaguely, that the evil was not having sex, but being part of this group, being forced to do it, having to prove that one is a man. Yet, he wanted nothing to be different, even if it hurt. Nothing that is may be subtracted, nothing in life can be thrown away.

Then he remembered the word "ritual". That is what it was, a ritual. The strange ritual of an exotic tribe.

OK, said Fisher, now do it. You first, Hans. He laughed: You know, what you do every night in your bed.

Hans asked, Why me? – but then looked vacantly into the bushes, started to tug at his penis, rubbing it, faster, his knees slightly bent, until the white semen ran over his fingers. Then the others formed a tight circle, and one after the other jerked off, while the rest watched. Most of them took a minute or less. Only De Rust worked and worked like mad, the others shouted encouragements, his face grew red, his dick was swollen and looked sore, and then he produced a few drops of the white substance, which excited them all so much.

Finally it was his turn. A few movements from the wrist, and his cock stood straight and his glans gained its full dark-purple colour. He jerked off twice. Hardly had he squirted the first full load white across the dark humus, when he started again. After a short time he splashed the same white load on top of the other which by now had dried up and seeped into the ground. The others laughed nervously, and applauded.

Fisher said: I wouldn't have thought you could do this. You always look so . . . well, prissy.

He hit Fisher with a hard fist, and Fisher looked at him incredulously, before he fought back. Things do not behave regularly, there are no things, there are no rules, there is no one-after-another. They rolled, naked on the black ground, punching and hitting furiously, while their genitals dangled and touched in a wild dance, and he kept thinking, Why do I do this, what is this all about, Fisher screaming all the time – Well, you are a sissy, but we are going to teach you, we are going to teach you, we are going to make a man of you yet. You bloody bookworm, you nerd, you think you can fuck us, screw us, look down on us, you, you . . . you wanker! Pain, too, is a kind of joy.

In the end, the others separated them, and they all raced through the thicket, their clothes in their hands, across to the farm dam, still naked, and jumped into the ice-cold and slightly dirty water. As he dived down into the dark depth of the dam, he washed off the afternoon's activities, he heard his breath escaping from his mouth, gurgling upwards towards the light, and he returned to the greenish brilliance broken like shards. He thought: I do not want to be mistaken, I do not want to be confused with them, even when I cannot escape them, even when I swim with them in this slimy farm dam. He somehow knew he was different from them, but he could not formulate how. When he rose out of the water, he saw Fisher swimming towards him, grinning. He started to crawl, and escaped to the bank, raced towards the trees and grabbed his clothes, ran into the thicket, but Fisher had lost interest, had jumped into the dam again, so he could dress and walk away from the noise of the boys in the water.

That night he dreamt of Fisher hunting him through the trees, they were both naked as they had been in the afternoon, naked they climbed the trees, in a hurried, febrile nakedness, squirting their seed into the rough bark, then Fisher started embracing him, and then mounting him, like he had seen a dog mount a bitch, screaming all the time, well, you are prissy, but we are going to teach you, we are going to teach you. You bloody bookworm, you think you can despise us, look down on us, you, you . . . and then he hit on the right phrase, he must have heard it somewhere – you, you, you bloody intellectual!

A moment of anxiety

HAVING A FAMILY IS AWFUL. Having to go on holiday with a family is sheer hell. When her parents went into the breakers, she was supposed to watch her little sisters. Both of them were real devils. Whenever she tried to read, they would throw sand over her book, or they would carefully put a wet jellyfish between her shoulder blades. She hated that. It made her body go pimply with distaste. Had she ever been as mindless as that herself? Surely not! She couldn't remember. She hated her sisters, and she couldn't stand her parents who made her watch them. In any case, they looked silly, half-naked in their swimsuits, her mother with her fat legs full of varicose veins, and her father with the thin spindly legs. They were just failures. Her mother always said that beauty is more than skin-deep, but nobody believed that kind of crap. You had to look good. Otherwise you didn't make it. And her mother and her father didn't look good. And when they went to swim they behaved like little children, splashing each other and ducking each other, embarrassing. Why couldn't they behave like bloody grown-ups once in a while?

In between their childish bouts in the water they smeared themselves with suncream and just lay there like two blobs, roasting in the sun. Sometimes at night she dreamt of murdering them both with a kitchen knife, blood spurting out of them. They understood nothing, not the music she wanted to play, they always complained that the music was too loud, and once her mother had even broken one of the records, saying that the music was satanic, that there were satanic words which, if one played the record backwards, would be like a black mass. Now, anybody knows that you cannot play a record backwards, and in any case, she got this out of one of her boring illustrated journals, where there were pictures of black candles and funny-shaped crosses and nonsense like that. They were such dupes. And they never understood her.

The worst was, of course, going on vacation with them. Nothing could be more boring than going on vacation with one's parents. And her parents were surely worse than anybody else's parents. She wasn't even allowed to go to a disco in the evening. They just sat in their hotel room and watched stupid TV all night. Her mother was constantly asking her what she was reading, and when she told her, always said the same thing: But Verena, don't you think that you are a bit too young for love stories? Too young, bloody hell. What did they know? They must have forgotten that they were young some time, at least one had to assume that. Everybody was young once. Even if she could not imagine her mother as a young girl. Was she always fat like she was now? If she was, she must have had a hell of a time. Her father was probably a sissy when he was her age. Well, just her luck, to have parents like that. She couldn't imagine them ever having been her age. Else, how could they have forgotten what it feels like? They now seemed to be so insensitive, as if they had always been "adults", "parents". Having a family is a real drag.

She got angry when her father said: Pull in your tummy. Your tummy is too fat. She didn't know what to say. She knew that if she said anything now it would come out all hateful and spoil the day. She did not want to have another row with her father right now. Words are slippery. You never say what you want to say. It always comes out differently. You get entangled in them, they ensnare you, you trip, and feel silly. How can anybody take you seriously, when your mouth forms words which are not your own? You can't even take yourself seriously. In the end she said nothing, and walked away in silence.

They are impossible. They never allow you to be. They always moan about this and about that. About your hair or your legs. About the way you walk or sit. Stand up straight, or you will never get a man. Nothing you do is ever right for them. About making noise when they want to sleep, about not wanting to wash the dishes. About dresses she was not allowed to wear, because they were too short, because, as her mother said, no Christian should wear something that was so sinful. She didn't know how dresses could be sinful. She hated her father, as she walked over the hot sand towards the dunes. I think they never wanted me in the first place. They didn't want a child then. Her mother had said this once to a friend when she had forgotten that she was in the other room where she could hear it. And now her tummy is too fat. They just didn't love her. They hated her. Well, she hated them back.

Why could one not come into this world as an adult, and forget about being a child, having to toe the line and be nice to one's parents? Why is there always so much pain? Mind you, other children seemed to have nice parents. Some of her friends' parents were really nice. But not her own. Somehow her past seemed to her to consist of little shards of glass, dangerous, sharp, broken. It was ashy, of the colour of ashes. Whenever she touched it, it hurt. It was better not to touch it. It was always the same. Things were hurting. People were hurting. Words were hurting. She felt miserable. When she looked down she saw that her tummy was too fat. But why did he have to say it? This was supposed to be a vacation, when people are joking and are happy. Not all this moaning.

There was a secret path, at least she called it the secret path, be-

cause nobody ever seemed to walk along that path, it started somewhere in the sand dunes as a mere gap in the shrubs, and then it
was weaving through the dune valley to the next, higher dune,
completely covered by trees of medium height. Once you reached
that point, the path was invisible from the beach. For her this was
a good place, but she felt courageous for walking through the dune
forest, vaguely thinking of the kind of dangers that were possible
once you left the road where everybody walked. Not so much wild
animals. Although she was not absolutely sure. There could be
leopards around still. But probably not. If her mother knew what
this place was like, she would be worried. She would definitely not
allow her to walk here alone. But there were these stories of girls
being molested. She thought the word "molested", but did not
quite know what happened when a girl was "molested". Something
awful, dirty. People warned her about it, but people did not talk
about it. It was something that happened if you walked alone at
night, of if you walked alone through unfamiliar parks. But she
didn't know what happened. It was like talking and at the same
time not talking.

Then she thought about witches, crooked old women, who
lured children into strange houses and cooked them in steaming
cauldrons, with a wart on their left nostril, and long greyish hair
streaming wildly in the wind, and how they lived in woods just
like these, but dismissed the idea as childish. She didn't after all
still believe in fairy tales. But one never knew.

But nothing happened.

The trees were opening up a bit, and the sun filtered through
the leaves. She must be near the other side of the dune forest,
where the sugar-cane fields started. It was then that she saw him.
He was about her age and her size. His shirt was torn, and his
trousers stained by oil. He moved nearly soundlessly on bare feet
between the tree trunks. Only now and then his feet broke a twig
with a slight cracking sound. He had seen her too.

For a moment they stood looking at each other, without moving. The boy was uncertain and made a movement as if to run away. She gasped, uncertain whether to be afraid or not. She decided there was no need. Although he was "black", he was not bigger than her, and while he seemed well built, she knew that she was as strong as he. He said something which she could not understand, it must be in Zulu, she thought. So she said: Hi! He grinned.

Then he moves towards her, he breaks the moment of stillness by moving towards her, she wants to scream, but there is nobody who will hear her, he opens his mouth again to smile and she is struck by his white, strong teeth, she sees an animal, they are all animals, her mother always said, they are all animals. She stands as if frozen to the ground, her heart thumping. Then, as he comes nearer, he again says something she cannot understand. Then he stands in front of her, and tugs at the strap of her swimsuit. Now she is afraid, and recoils from him.

But he laughs. He tears off his shirt, and his trousers, he suddenly stands naked in the shadowy green of the dune forest and is silent, and there is this hush, no bird screeches, only very far off there is the nearly inaudible sound of the sea breaking against the beach where her parents wait for her. She looks at the naked boy, she forgets that she is afraid, he is beautiful without the tattered trousers and shirt full of tears, he is beautiful in the dark brown colour of his strong limbs and his black, woolly hair.

She remembered phrases from her love stories: "He looked deep into her eyes", and she thought he was doing this right now, only that the lovers in her book had never been naked black boys of her own age, but respectable men in business suits who had a car and who took you to dinner and to dancing afterwards, and who were rewarded with a kiss, and then she remembered the phrase "she felt her heart flutter", and that was what was happening to her at this moment, and she thought that she must be in love, but this boy was black, and you couldn't be in love with a black boy, and then she thought, "the blood drained from her face", but she did not know how to do that. But it happened to her anyway: and there was the fear again, what would this crazy naked boy do to her, would he "molest" her, whatever that was. She suddenly knew that she had stepped into a place the rules of which were foreign to her. It was a difficult, a dangerous place, even perhaps a deadly place. It was now no longer possible for her to imagine the ending of this story, the love stories had no rules for this encounter on the secret path.

The boy was still grinning and again tried to tug at her strap, but she evaded him. Then she understood what he meant, and she slowly peeled the swimsuit from her body, pudgy with puppy fat, but flat as a board, as her classmates used to say, but surely they had never experienced real love, where you confront each other naked, and she knew that that was how it had to be. And, of course, he was eyeing the place where she should have had breasts and then the place between her legs, all the girls in her class had said that's all boys are interested in. The girls were always talking about their figures and how she was underdeveloped for her age. To her face they called it slim, but that was not what they meant, they meant that she was "underdeveloped", had not grown breasts, and that her tummy was too fat. But now she did not mind. It was a kind of a sacred moment here in the forest, and nothing mattered but his eyes on her.

At first they moved around each other, awkward, shy, at arm's length, then they chased each other through the trees and the undergrowth, she had lost all fear, she did not notice how the twigs scratched her legs and her arms, they were laughing like children engrossed in a game, their bodies moving, propelled by a graceful force, whirling, sliding, flashes of pink and brown in the green of the forest.

Then suddenly she raced back towards the beach, along her secret path, not even looking around to see if the boy followed her. She followed the path up the dune, she heard his breathing behind her, racing down, they left the cover of the forest, the low scrub around them became sparse, and then they raced, still laughing across the last sand dune, they burst through the gap in the shrubs on to the beach, when she noticed her parents, her father getting up, her mother screaming, but her scream remained mute, the sound of the sea swallowed it, her father on his funny spindly legs racing towards her. She stopped, saw how the boy, sudden fright in his face, turned, ran away, as her father came towards her, shouting, angry, ran past her towards the point in the scrub where the boy had disappeared, the figure of her father, too, disappeared in the scrub. And down there at the beach, her mother was still screaming soundlessly in the noise of the surf, and as she turned to walk down to her, she suddenly noticed that she was still naked.